BLAME ME

PAULA ASTRIDGE

Distributed in Australia by:
Woodslane Press Pty Ltd
10 Apollo Street
Warriewood NSW 2102
Email: info@woodslane.com.au
Tel: 02 8445 2300 Website: www.woodslane.com.au

First published in Australia in 2026 by Rowell41

A catalogue record for this book is available from the National Library of Australia

Printed in Australia
Design by: The Mighty Pen @mightythepen

For my father,

Major (Dr.) Esmond C. Smith

Australian Army Medical Corps (AAMC)

Kokoda and Sananada Trails.

OTHER BOOKS BY PAULA ASTRIDGE

Kill the Fuhrer

Golden Boy

In the Way of the Reich

Waltzing Dixie

Bad Hand

Scallywag

Rocket Man

Deep Sleep

Because Our Fathers Lied

God bless America.

God save the Queen.

God defend New Zealand

And thank Christ for Australia.

– Russell Crowe

BLAME ME

PROLOGUE

NO ONE CALLS AUSTRALIAN SOLDIERS COWARDS and gets away with it. Least of all, their own Commander-in-Chief, General Thomas Blamey, who was branded as one himself during the Greek Campaign of 1941.

The WWII operation was lost even before it began, but bent on pursuing it, the British thrust Australian troops into a re-run of The Great War's Gallipoli, This time, with odds stacked so overwhelmingly against them that there was finally no option but full retreat with the German juggernaut thundering towards them.

Yet, while they withdrew south with small bands of their men making suicidal stands to protect their mates' backs, Blamey jumped on a plane to Egypt and winged his way to safety, leaving Greece and his troops to their fate.

More than 700 Australians died or were wounded, and while over 5000 were taken prisoner, those lucky to elude capture had weeks of hell ahead with every man for himself risking life and limb to fight his own way home.

Blamey would never be forgiven for that, but those who knew him better said in his defence:

"He's no coward. Just a man who knows what he wants and stops at nothing to get it."

What Blamey wanted, at that point, was the promotion the British promised him on the proviso that he leave Greece immediately and fly to Cairo's Allied Headquarters.

There, to be made the Deputy Commander-in-Chief of Middle East Command; a title the British trumped-up to stop him being so bloody-minded about what was best for his Australian troops. Forever insisting, as he did, that they fight as one and not be broken up and spread thin, when it served Britain's purpose to do just that.

It was a delicate situation that risked ruining relations between Britain and Australia, so the only way they could side-line Blamey without causing offence was to pander to his ego with this brand new job. One, which beyond its bells and whistles, had no significance and was as pointless as the Greek Campaign itself.

But Blamey was no fool, and seeing it for what it was, took shameless advantage of it as his fastest way to the top. A place he intended to stay for the rest of his life. If not always with the support of those of his peers who loathed him, then by actively sabotaging the career of any general, who by way of superior performance, threatened to topple him from his pedestal.

No one ever did, because Blamey was a survivor – a man of outstanding intelligence, initiative and endurance, who successfully shifted the emphasis from his shady private life to play a star role in two world wars; all the while, fighting his way through far worse on the brutal battlefields of government and military politics.

Many believe that, for all Blamey's bad, there was much about him that was good and that he was first and foremost for Australia.

Yet 80 years on from the Second World War others still say: "*What rot!* Blamey was first and foremost for himself from the beginning."

BLAME ME

PART ONE

THE KIND OF MEN WHO WORE KHAKI

BLAME ME

CHAPTER 1

RECRUITMENT OFFICER TUBMAN SCOFFED when the underage applicant came to sign up.

"Run home to your mother boy, and don't come back until you're fully grown."

His words raised a laugh all round, and as the butt of the joke, young Tom Blamey strode from the enrolment hall – his face, with its dark determined brows and compelling pale eyes, burning with rage and humiliation.

"What's bloody well wrong with being fifteen," he cursed out loud as he went, "when I'm better than any man here!"

It was a boast backed by the fact that Tom Blamey could run rings around anyone when it came to the bush and horse-riding skills his father had taught him, while he already had a reputation as a 'crack shot'.

As for being fully grown – well he already was, with a sturdy 5' 6½" build, that as stubborn as Blamey himself, refused to budge an inch.

All of it made him so angry. Here it was, near the turn of the twentieth century, and desperate to break free from the obscurity of being just one of ten children and the son of a local farmer, he had thought that the 1899 Boer War call to arms was his sure-fire way of distinguishing himself.

It wasn't, and apart from being disappointed, he was ashamed of trying to distance himself from his father, who worked every hour of the day to support his family on his twenty acres of land. However, love and admire that father as he did, Tom had no intention of following in his footsteps and was set on taking far greater strides into the future.

To that end, he knew he'd get over the shame of this day, which was more than could be said for Officer Tubman, who'd never forget having turned away the man who was to become Australia's most celebrated soldier: the first and only one to reach the rank of Field Marshal.

Before Blamey marched into the fray, however, he had to settle for something a little less stellar as a trainee teacher in Lake Albert, a small suburb built on what was once a swamp, in the New South Wales town of Wagga.

"He's strict, but fair," the school's rough little gang of students agreed during his two-year tenure there.

They were two years that Blamey put to good use; in between all the reading, writing and arithmetic, refining what would become his method of operation for the rest of his career.

"A bit of the fear factor doesn't hurt," he told his family. "Kids are exactly like the brumbies we break here on the farm. Show them who's boss from the beginning, but temper it with a bit of good humour."

It was his failure to adhere to his own advice, unfortunately, that had him leave the school on a sour note. Not due to the headmaster, who always thought the best of him, but to the allegation that Blamey had lost control and taken it out on a student.

A mistake he made worse by denying it.

Student-teachers such as he were forbidden to discipline pupils by physical means and, in compliance, Blamey kept his hot temper on hold until the last days of term, when after being endlessly patient with one slow learner, he suddenly snapped and struck the boy a blow. He had no excuse other than the fact that 12-year-old Jimmy Seckold pushed him too far.

"I don't understand, sir.... please explain it again," Seckold said, baiting Blamey for the amusement of his mates by asking him to repeat what he'd already made clear ten times over.

Blamey wasn't a man to be mocked, and with his blood on boil and beyond seeing reason, he lashed out with his ruler, leaving a bright red brand across the boy's cheek.

The boy's father didn't like the look of it and went straight to the school's Headmaster Kimber to complain.

"My son said that Blamey hit him, and that his mate, Freddie Brunskill here, saw him do it."

Freckle-faced Brunskill, in his shabby uniform, was cowering in the corner of Kimber's office wishing that he hadn't volunteered as a witness, because no matter which way it went, it didn't bode well with the headmaster's eyes now hard on him.

"Did you see Mr Blamey hit your friend?" Kimber demanded.

In a flash of terror, Brunskill baulked before answering:

"Yes sir. Mr Blamey hit him with a ruler."

It was as simple as that and Brunskill was sent on his way.

That wasn't so bad, the boy thought, as he walked back down the school corridor.

It seemed he'd been let off the hook, so it came as a shock

when he was summoned back to the office the next day. There, to say again what he'd said before, not only to the headmaster, but to the very man he had accused. As he stood on trembling legs before the big desk, both Blamey and Kimber, sitting behind it, were glaring at him like black-capped judges of the Inquisition.

The headmaster spoke:

"Did you, Master Brunskill, see Mr Blamey strike Jimmy Seckold?"

"Yes sir."

His prompt response had the headmaster turn to his student-teacher, but Blamey said without batting an eye:

"I did not hit the boy."

Kimber took him at his word, and believing Blamey to be incapable of telling such a bald-faced lie, swung round more savagely on Brunskill.

"Do you hear that boy? Do you still insist that you saw Mr. Blamey strike Seckold?"

"Yes sir, I did," the boy braved with waning courage.

It was at this point that Kimber lost patience.

"Now look here!" he barked back. "If you weren't a new boy at the school I'd give you a sound thrashing. Why are you telling such tales?"

"But I *did* see it him do it, sir... *I did!*"

Brunskill was on the brink of tears and near crumbling under the men's fearsome scowls, but being torn between the prospect of the headmaster's cane or the belting he'd get at home for telling a lie, he opted for the lesser of two evils and persisted with the truth.

It was a stalemate, and with frustration on both sides, the boy was finally sent back to class, leaving Kimber to wonder as he watched him go.

"Never mind, boys will be boys," he said, giving Blamey the benefit of the doubt with a pat on the back, while pretending not to see what had just shown up as the other side of his seemingly sterling character.

Blamey, for his part, was prepared to forget the whole incident. It crossed his mind that a man of better conscience and courage would have put the child out of his misery by admitting to fault, hut having weighed up his options, he'd decided against it and was relieved that all ill-feeling was forgotten when fate put its foot in the door.

CHAPTER 2

"I'VE BEEN OFFERED A POSITION in Western Australia," he announced proudly to his family. "They want me to teach at Fremantle Boys' School."

It was a huge compliment and, in response, Blamey moved like lightning. Within days he had said goodbye to all he'd known and taken himself, along with his hopes, to the other side of the country. While Lake Albert had been a good place to get his feet wet, his eyes were on the main chance and, relatively speaking, this opportunity was like exchanging Outback for Oxford.

The school had an excellent reputation, and as the best The West could offer, Blamey was to give it his all, taking its motto: *Play the Game* to heart and carrying its cryptic meaning as his standard until the day he died.

To work in the big city, however, meant change. Rather than ride his horse to school in simple clothes and straw hat, it was now transit by tram sporting stiff collar, formal dark suit and demeanour. Yet in essence, he stayed the same, sticking to his guns as a hard, but popular taskmaster, while going above and beyond by training the cadet shooting team so well that it won the Western Australia Cup.

"How did you do it?" he was asked by those who believed that the school's strength lay in scholastics, not sport.

"Discipline," Blamey replied, running his finger round the rim of his tight collar.

"Which I owe entirely to my strict Methodist upbringing."

Though he intended it as a joke, it was taken seriously and he soon found himself ensconced in the church community. Not merely as a member, but as a lay preacher and leading light. It didn't take him long to latch on to the benefits of belonging to the right social set, so he threw himself into it with a new-found enthusiasm for God based less on religious zeal than seeing it as the perfect platform to put himself centre stage and hold the public in the palm of his hand.

"He's an impressive young chap," one parishioner commented to another after Sunday service. "He has such presence and power of persuasion. Are you sure he's only 20?"

Within five weeks, in fact, he was to turn 22, but what were a couple of years in terms of his achievements? Blamey's were so exceptional that, within days of that 22nd birthday, the Methodist church appointed him as their associate minister in the port town of Carnarvon.

He couldn't have been more flattered, but it wasn't where he wanted to stay, and soon after, on seeing the Australian Military's advertisement in Perth's *West Australian* newspaper, he knew exactly where he wanted to go. Its call for men to join the service took up two columns and was offering commissions on their new Cadet Instructional Staff to young men of good calibre. It was a career path that had Blamey's name written all over it.

The deadline for the entrance exam was only 12 days away,

which seemed short notice, but when Blamey flipped to the front page, he was even more alarmed to find that the paper was already a week old.

There was no time to lose. He had to cram into a few days what should have been learnt in a year. So he put his head down, and as if his life depended on it, studied like a demon, burning the midnight oil, barely eating or sleeping, until with dark-ringed eyes and every bone in his body aching, he presented himself at the examination hall, picked up his pen, and put his name at the top of the test paper.

"I came third in Australia!" he announced to all who'd listen when the results came out.

They were exemplary compared to those of the host of other candidates, and it went without saying that he'd secured one of the coveted positions. Certainly he should have, but that wasn't the way the military worked, and the letter sent from its Melbourne headquarters didn't let him down gently:

> *We would like to congratulate you on your outstanding results. Unfortunately, we cannot offer you a position, because there are none available in Western Australia.*

"*WHAT!*" Blamey let out, unable to believe it. "I've been rejected because preference has gone to the eastern states."

It was flagrantly unfair, and refusing to lie down under it, he went straight to his desk, and with what was to become his trademark gall, wrote back to the man in charge, demanding his rights.

Dear Major Bruche,
I'm not disappointed – I'm furious! It is an outrage that having achieved 3rd place, I've been denied a commission when other men in the east, whose results were far worse, are being measured up for their lieutenant's uniforms.

Major Julius Bruche, Deputy Assistant Adjutant-General, wrote back:

We are sorry there are no vacancies in Western Australia. May we suggest you curb your enthusiasm until there are.

Blamey, however, wasn't defeated and sent a response every bit as dispassionate, taking care not to be discourteous, but dropping mention of the legal and moral ramifications of his claim.

As an ex-barrister, Bruche cocked a cynical eyebrow when he read it.

"Well at least this young fellow is a fighter," he said, more impressed than put out by Blamey's veiled threat of taking legal action, and the fact that he'd done it so skilfully.

There was some satisfaction for Bruche when he wrote his note of surrender:

You shall have your commission young man. Please report to the old Navy drill hall in Port Melbourne on November 1.

It was out of pure curiosity that Bruche was there to greet him.

"So you're the aggressive young cub who caused such a hubbub at Victoria Barracks," he said as soon as he set eyes on him. "Who did you get to write that threatening letter – a lawyer?"

"No sir," the freshly-inducted Lieutenant Blamey answered. "They were my words."

"I doubt it," Bruche mumbled smugly as he walked away, because he was sure that the letter's professional jargon couldn't have possibly been crafted by one without legal training. Yet, in the years to come, Bruche was to learn that such workmanship and resolute will was completely consistent with the man Blamey was and would ever be.

CHAPTER 3

BY THE TIME BLAMEY RETURNED from his staff officer training at Pakistan's Quetta College, he had not only fallen on his feet, but in love. At least he thought he had.

If he could get beyond his preference for buxom blondes, he was sure that Millie Millard, with her black, curly hair, trim figure and good breeding was by far the best looking girl in Melbourne's Methodist community. Her admirable dedication to the church and cheerful ways made her a most suitable future wife for an up and coming army officer, a commendable woman on whom he could rely to raise his children with minimum input from him. For even now, Blamey knew that he would never be a family man – that his only devotion was to himself and the impact he was determined to make on the Australian military.

Their white wedding was followed by their first house. A quaint cottage, which on his captain's pay wasn't so impressive, but with it being within range of reflecting the wealth of Millie's family home in Toorak, Blamey was well on his way to the world being his oyster. He didn't know that he was going to be given a run for his money; that a man, one year his junior, was on the up-and-up and equally dogged about making his mark.

John Lavarack, Blamey would always say, was a 'silver-spooner', someone who was served life on a platter and for whom he had less regard than for men like himself who had to rise through the ranks the hard way.

It helped to dismiss Lavarack like this, because everything about him put Blamey's feral instincts on alert, sparking competition and a much-resented jealousy that Blamey preferred to call disdain. It was a contempt that would flourish into a life-time feud between them with Blamey making it his business to rob Lavarack of any opportunity that might see his star rise above his own. It was easy to do given Blamey's senior rank, but over the years, Lavarack was never to let up, and by WWII, Blamey wouldn't be sure whether it was better to hold the upper hand over him or Hitler.

The trouble began back in the beginning when Blamey misread Lavarack's personal profile. For where platters and spoons were concerned, Lavarack's were merely silver-plated with a background not nearly as privileged as Blamey presumed. Despite his imposing presence and eloquence, Lavarack came into the world without fanfare, born in Brisbane to British parents of little social sway, and in the company of two siblings, who had less in common with him than Blamey.

He and Blamey were, in fact, a matching pair, but were too headstrong and vain to admit it. Both sharing the same drive and dedication to the cause, but with different ways of serving it that stopped them ever seeing eye to eye. Though Blamey would be happy to concede that Lavarack was better looking and had six inches on him in height, that was as far as he'd go in giving the man a compliment when the force of their respective magnetic fields made it a case of like poles repelling.

There was just one thing on which they agreed: Neither liked losing – the fine line between being the lengths to which one of them was prepared to go to ensure that he didn't.

–oOo–

"Ninety-eight percent!" 20-year-old Lavarack reported to his father when he received the exam results for a commission in the Permanent Military Forces. It was 1905 and it was official. He was now a lieutenant in the Royal Australian Artillery.

His father, Major Cecil Lavarack of the Queensland Defense Force, wasn't surprised when he expected no less of his son who had excelled at school and at everything else he set out to achieve.

The military was in their blood, and he was so proud to see his son standing before him now – tall, dark and handsome, with his electric blue eyes and incisive mind ready to take on the world. Of course, being British, the major would never say as much, and didn't need to when his son was never slow in coming forward and was already fully aware that he was rather exceptional.

"I'm glad it all worked out this way," the major said instead, "with you going into the military instead of medicine."

It had been a sore point for John, having to put aside his aspirations of becoming a doctor, but with his older sister studying to be the same and his parents unable to afford the extra tuition, he'd had no choice. Yet now, he wasn't sorry at all to be swapping stethoscope for sword, because he'd seen a brighter path ahead and had already hit the ground running.

Like Blamey, he had reached the rank of captain by 1913, and having secured the privilege of staff officer training at the elite Camberley College in Surrey, he and his beautiful, new hazel-eyed bride, Sybil, were off to England.

It should have been a two-year course, but a few months before its conclusion, WWI spoiled the fun. There had been a great deal of it before then, squeezed in between the strict protocol and training, with the dazzling Captain and Mrs Lavarack starring at every military dinner party and ball. All of it had gone to their heads, as did that one drink too many that Lavarack had at the Sandhurst vs Camberley Cricket Final celebrations.

He had hit for six and saved the day, and while being hoisted triumphantly onto his teammates' shoulders, had swilled a trophy full of beer. Normally, as a man ever cool and collected, he held his liquor well, but on this night of August 4, 1914, he found himself slumped between two fellow officers as they wobbled their way back to base.

The guards on the gates were usually good sports, but for some reason, this time, they were vigilant and in no mood to tolerate them breaking the rules.

"You're drunk, you've missed curfew, and shall all be put on report," one of them snapped when he saw Lavarack, with peaked cap askew, leaning heavily on his companions for support.

"Have a heart Sarge," one of those propping him up pleaded, before offering the perfect explanation: "He's Australian!"

With no more needing to be said, the sentry excused from a colonial what would never be accepted as best of British behavior and answered sternly:

"Well sober him up, and do it fast, because as of an hour ago, we are at war!"

Due to the dire circumstances, Lavarack's one-off indiscretion was forgotten, for Austria's Archduke Franz Ferdinand had been shot at Sarajevo and the world would never be the same.

CHAPTER 4

WHEN THE BRITISH DECLARED WAR it was assumed that Australians would be right there with them, fighting not so much at their side, but as frontline expendables. Those who had fought and survived the Second Boer War weren't so keen, but the host of untried men from southern shores saw it as their free ticket to see the world and couldn't wait.

Lavarack and Blamey had a head start, because they were already in London. The war had closed Camberley College, and due to high demand for staff officers, its students had been fast-tracked and were spread thin in their speedy allocation to army divisions. As one of the most promising among them, Lavarack was stationed at the British War Office, which would have been a lonely place for his foreign feet to wander had there not been one other Australian doing the same.

–oOo–

> *Good news twice over,* Blamey wrote home to his wife. *I've been promoted to major and am transferring to the British War Office where I'll be working in the Intelligence Branch preparing daily summaries for the King and the Secretary of State for War, Lord Kitchener.*

It was a wonderful opportunity, and with him having been recalled back to Britain from Australia to serve on the staff of the Wessex Division, it was one he wasn't about to miss. While excitedly scribbling the details down for his wife, however, the ink in his pen ran out and, in frustration, he hurled it across the room.

What he would have written, had it still been inked-up and in hand, was that the war, so far, was treating him well; because fully-trained staff officers were in such short supply. As a result, while in Britain, he had been appointed to the Australian Imperial Force as General Staff Officer, Grade 3 for Major General William Bridges' 1st Division. There to report to the most brilliant man of the day – it's GSO1, Lieutenant Colonel Brudenell White.

What more could a man climbing the military ladder want? Blamey thought, before he was granted the further boon of fighting the war shoulder-to-shoulder with WWI's greatest commander – General John Monash.

He would learn from the best, but with such men as Monash and White taking him under their wing, it could only be wondered whether the mistakes Blamey was to make in WWII were because he had forgotten or willfully disregarded what they taught him.

In November, he sailed from England in stellar company. He and Australia's renowned Colonel Harry Chauvel sharing the view and a couple of cigars on the ship's deck while on their way to join their Australian contingent in Egypt.

"It's such an exciting time," Blamey said, gazing wistfully into the Mediterranean night.

They were words of youth and inexperience that Chauvel couldn't answer. Instead, he took a final puff of his cigar, and discarding its burning embers into the sea, said goodnight. It was the fastest way to quit the conversation and spare Blamey the truth – that there was nothing, whatsoever, exciting about war, and that in his own anticipation of it, Chauvel's whole being was in recoil, for he had fought the battles of the Boer War and knew what hell lay ahead.

Blamey would find out for himself on April 25, 1915, because Winston Churchill, as First Lord of the Admiralty, had set his sights on taking Constantinople and wanted to kick off the campaign at a little place called Gallipoli.

As part of the offensive, Blamey was on board the battleship *HMS Prince of Wales*, which after anchoring off Turkey's coast, had disgorged Australia's 10th Battalion and wasn't weighing so low in the water. Much like the rest of the convoy that had been relieved of its cargo by rolling out onto the beach waves of Australian and New Zealand troops, who had gone forth, blind to their fate, in the pitch black of pre-dawn.

The sun, since then, had risen and was affording a splendid view of the white sands now running red with their blood. Those still aboard ship were struck dumb, and at the sickening realisation that theirs was a suicide mission, moved to their stations in silence.

It wasn't until Major General Bridges and the staff from his 1st Division clambered down the ship's ladder into the waiting trawler that someone spoke:

"What's the time? "Lieutenant Colonel White asked.

Blamey looked at his watch.

"7.20, sir," he answered, as he steadied himself against the waves buffeting their boat, and the fact that none on board gave a tinker's cuss for their chances now that they'd found out that their entire force had been landed in the wrong place.

"About a mile and a half from the designated beach," British Naval Command informed Bridges, before adding defensively: "Couldn't be helped. Our sailors were disorientated in the dark and veered a little left."

It was a slight deviation from plan that cost thousands of Australian lives.

Their 10th Battalion struck out at 4.00am as scouts and first to the slaughter; soon to be followed by 16,000 Australian and New Zealand troops on a mission to storm the beach and push inland as fast as possible. Yet even before they reached shore, the Turks spotted them and opened fire, riddling their rowboats and those aboard with bullet holes that soon oozed blood and brine.

For those among them who were fresh to war it came as a shock to see their best mates being blown to bits beside them. So they stopped looking left or right and stared straight ahead with gritted teeth and white-knuckled hands clenched tight to the gunwales. The second they hit dry land they leapt out, but in the mayhem many dropped into deep water and drowned, while the stronger swimmers among them struggled to reach shore, fighting to keep their heads above water with machine-gun fire whipping around them and their water-logged packs dragging them down.

"Where in the hell are we?" Private Arthur Blackburn[1] called out in the confusion when his feet finally touched solid ground.

As to that, his commanding officer, Lieutenant Talbot Smith[2] had no answer, for they' had been trained to fight on flat terrain and here looming before them on the beach were sheer, close-to-unclimbable cliffs. He and his troops were in a state of dismay, and with the Turks' gunfire not letting up, Talbot knew that it was surely only the emergency of the moment that gave him the courage to shout:

"Come on boys. They can't hit you. Are you ready?"

He then led the way straight up the rocks, while those who followed behind, burdened by full kits, clung on for grim death. The only way they could do it was to dig their bayonets into the earth for handholds while keeping their heads low in the hope of avoiding the hail of enemy bullets. It didn't work, for although the Turks couldn't target their kill in the dark, their random shots reaped rich reward.

If not hit, many of the soldiers climbing the cliffs lost their grip and tumbled to their death, while one by one, those killed or wounded, slid back down the slope until their bodies came to a stop in the tangle of wild scrub below. Somehow, however, hundreds of them made it to the top, the first of whom quickly disposed of the Turks causing the trouble and cleared the way for the rest of the Anzac troops to scramble up and over and get inland fast.

It was a triumph in itself for those men to set foot on the peak's plateau, but it wasn't until they caught their breath and looked around that they saw what they were really up against. Spread out before them was a whole new kind of enemy ready to take them on – a rugged landscape with craggy ridges and deep, impenetrable valleys stretching southward to the distant, imposing summits of the peninsula.

Their mission seemed impossible, and was made more so because they hadn't reckoned on the Turks being so fierce and coming equipped with a mindset to stand and fight at all costs.

By mid-morning, all benefits of the Anzac surprise attack had been lost, for just when they thought they were making headway in whittling down the resistance, more Turkish reinforcements arrived. Their sheer number was daunting, but worse was that they came under the command of Lieutenant Colonel Mustafa Kemal – a soldier of heroic repute, who believed that he and his troops were dispensable and destined to fight to the bitter end.

"I don't order you to attack. I order you to *die!*" he told his men before battle.[3]

"In the time it takes us to do it, other troops will be here to take our place."

Australians rarely faced an enemy with a resolve that matched their own, and this time they weren't to win, for they were fighting a futile battle on unfamiliar ground, where right from the first, they didn't stand a chance.

"The speed that the Turks are propelling their reserves onto the battlefield is killing us,"[4] one commander, speaking for the rest, reported to 1st Division Headquarters.

Their Anzac troops had made every effort to move inland, but most were stuck in a deadly stalemate with their backs to the sea. Like doomed gladiators in an arena, the Turks were looking down on those still on the beach from their ringside seats, watching them die for no reason at all, other than to later have the small strip of land on which they fell renamed Anzac Cove in their honour.

That cove was now jam-packed with the dead and writhing wounded. Soldiers Injured, but still standing, were stumbling their way to shelter, while the screams of those closer to death and being carried from the front, could barely be heard above the relentless rattle of Turkish machine-gun fire.

Commander of 1st Division, Bridges, was headquartered at the hub of it and could see the situation was hopeless.

"Come on,' he said to the Commander of the Anzacs, General William Birdwood. "Let's save what's left of our men."

To that end, they set out by trawler for the battleship *HMS Queen Elizabeth*, where the campaign's Commander-in-Chief, English General Sir Ian Hamilton, was sleeping safe and sound in his bunk.

"This is madness!," Bridges said the second he woke. "Our Allied troops are being massacred and can't meet their objectives. They must be withdrawn."

It was a rude awakening for Hamilton, but after clearing his groggy head, he conferred with his naval commanders and said:

"Instant evacuation is impossible. But don't worry. You've got through the worst of the bad business. Now all your men have to do is dig, dig, dig, until they are safe."

The Anzacs followed his orders and held on for that first crucial night, but by morning, more than 2000 of them were dead.

CHAPTER 5

IT WASN'T A STAFF OFFICER'S DUTY to distinguish himself in battle, but unable to simply stand by and watch the slaughter, Blamey stepped up. His first mission saw him sent to Gallipoli's Plateau 400 to evaluate the need for reinforcements there.[5]

"Colonel McCay's 2nd Brigade is desperate for them," he returned to headquarters to report.

He saluted Bridges and White looking the worse for wear with the pristine uniform in which he'd set out now caked in blood and dirt. Yet far from being shaken by the death-defying experience of making his way there and back, Blamey's jaw was set in determination, for he'd seen what his fellow soldiers were suffering and wanted to help them in any way he could.

Since their Anzac landing four days before, McCay and his 2nd Brigade had been stationed at Plateau 400 – an elevated plain named for its height above sea level, on which they had been told to 'hold the high ground'. As a result, a thousand of McCay's men were dead, and although McCay, himself, had escaped death three times over, with one bullet penetrating his peaked cap, and another slicing through his sleeve, a third had hit him in the leg. It wasn't enough to stop him taking the field, but by the time Blamey arrived to monitor their situation, McCay had lost a lot of blood, and barely able to walk, was in dire need of support.

Major General Bridges had to be careful in giving it:

"I want you to speak to me, not as subordinate to general, but as man to man,"[6] he phoned McCay at the front to say. "I have only one battalion left. Can you assure me that your need for it is absolute?"

McCay answered 'yes', and because Blamey had just returned from the front to confirm it, Bridges sent his final 4th Battalion and ordered Blamey to go with it.

"At least you know the way," Bridges cajoled to make light of him having to do a second run so soon, and Blamey, hiding his fear and exhaustion, smiled back.

He had to put both aside as he led the battalion up from the beach and through the battlefield; It was dangerous, hard going, and it wasn't until dusk that they reached the ridge being held by the handful of men McCay had left.

"By crikey, it's good to see you!" one of them said, because Blamey and the 4th had arrived in the nick of time to stop the Turks in their tracks.

With the onus now on the men of that 4th Battalion, they made a good show of it, one which they would later repeat when leading the successful charge at the Battle of Lone Pine. But in the meantime, all those who had been rescued on Plateau 400 called Blamey a hero, for he had played the role well and was soon to follow it up with a second act.

"I'll go," he volunteered when Bridges had to send out a small patrol to locate the battery of Turkish guns harassing the beach from their hidden vantage point at Olive Grove.

Those guns, not-so-affectionately nicknamed "Beachy Bill", were causing havoc.

In between taking potshots at the men risking a swim in the sea, they were cutting vital supply lines by firing on every Allied transport coming in and out of the cove. Warships were on their way to take care of them, but they needed a precise location to target.

With this in mind, Bridges looked long and hard at Blamey.

"Good!" he then answered, because he knew Blamey would do his best to get the job done. "Take Sergeant Wills and Bombardier Orchard with you."

They were to go deep behind enemy lines in the dead of night, and though their camouflage and the heavy cloud cover helped, right at the strategic moment those clouds moved from the moon, leaving them, for a split second, standing like stunned deer in the headlights, fair and square in front of the enemy.

"*Jesus!*" Orchard let out when they found themselves confronted by a party of Turks wielding bayoneted rifles.

One of them lunged at Orchard, and would have killed him had Blamey, with his skill as a marksman, not fired his pistol first. The Turk fell dead at Orchard's feet, and before his companions had time to react, Blamey and his two men made short work of them.

Orchard would never forget that Blamey saved his life; and for doing so, Blamey was mentioned in dispatches.

"You should be proud," Colonel White told him.

But to this, Blamey could only say with a shrug: "I'd be a whole lot prouder if I hadn't had to withdraw my patrol before finding the guns."

As far as he was concerned, his performance had been second-rate compared to that of the 10th Battalion's Private Philip Robins and Lance Corporal Arthur Blackburn, who as the first men to set foot on Gallipoli's sands, had put on an astounding show of courage by penetrating further inland than any other Australian.

Robins was killed three days later, which meant his efforts went unrewarded, but Blamey would never forget Blackburn's name, for he was to live on and fight under his command during WWII. By then, Blackburn would be a Brigadier, because now, in WWI, he was about to win the Victoria Cross at the Battle of Pozieres.

The small town in Northern France was just a tiny speck on the face of the Earth, but it was to play one of the biggest and bloodiest parts in the Battle of the Somme. It was to be among Australia's first major offensives on the Western Front, and Blackburn, along with Blamey and Brigade Major John Lavarack, would be there to fight it out.

CHAPTER 6

LAVARACK HAD BEEN CHAMPING AT THE BIT to be in the action. Although he'd been assigned to the AIF from the start, his many requests to be moved to the Western Front had been ignored, and it wasn't until he joined Australia's 2nd Division in 1916 that he got what he wanted.

"I should have been more careful about what I wished for," he thought when standing in the midst of Pozieres' carnage. It made him feel sick and he couldn't imagine why he'd been in such an all-fired hurry to make himself a part of it.

He, with the rest of the 2nd Division, had arrived to relieve Australia's 1st, whose men had seized the German front and taken the town with relative ease. Theirs would be a hard act to follow. But before the battle began, that outcome hadn't been so certain.

–oOo–

"We've been ordered to attack tomorrow night, but that's not going to happen," the Commander of Australia's 1st Division, Major General Harold Walker, had said to Blamey as he peered through his binoculars at the small village of Pozieres set as their target.

There was defiance in Walker's tone, because that order had come from the controversial Commander of Britain's 5th Army, General Hubert Gough, whose meteoric rise through the ranks hadn't come by way of merit, but by being one of Field Marshal Douglas Haig's best friends. As the Commander-in-Chief of the British forces in France, Haig was the top dog and had to be obeyed, as did his direct subordinates, but Gough's poor military moves in the past, together with his reputation as a dangerous 'thruster', put his fellow generals on edge.

"It's the wrong move and will risk too many lives," Walker then went on to say to Blamey, because he'd received the directive as soon as his division arrived on site and he knew it was premature.

Like his predecessor, General Bridges, who'd been fatally wounded fighting in the trenches at Gallipoli, Walker's priority was always his men, and despite the fact that he was British, all the Anzacs under his command loved and admired him for it.

No one more so than Blamey, who as his GSO1, asked tentatively:

"Well, what did you tell Gough?"

He and Walker always got on well, so he felt free to ask, but this time, his senior officer's offhand response, made him baulk:

"I told him to take a flying leap!"

The look of surprise on Blamey's face forced Walker to fill him in:

"I told him to forget taking shortcuts ... that this time, if we wanted to win, there'd be no skipping preparations."

It was the right call, for five days later, with his men all geared up to go, Walker led the way to the first success in what had been a series of Allied fiascos on the Western Front.

Their victory didn't sit well with the Germans. Defeat, for them, was bad enough, but to be beaten by the forces of such a small country with its hereto unheard of army was a humiliation that couldn't go unpunished. The best way they could do it was to turn the full might of their big guns on the Australian troops occupying the village with the intent of blasting both into oblivion.

–oOo–

This marked the point when Pozieres became the toughest task taken on by the AIF during the entire war, with its much-fought-for ridge destined to go down in history as being 'more densely sown with Australian sacrifice than any other place on Earth.'[7]

In less than seven weeks, more of its men would be wounded or killed than during the entire eight months at Gallipoli: 6,800 dead and 16.200 wounded – and all for the sake of a small windmill sitting on a hill.

That hill gave its 13th century windmill the best view of the Somme Valley, and since the beginning, had been the perfect stronghold from which the Germans could see, and guard against, all enemy movements. To date, it was the most coveted prize in the war, but to win it, thousands of Australians had to die and have their unidentified bodies buried beneath it. At the very least, the stone structure should have served as their tombstone, but it too would be reduced to rubble, leaving their remains to rot for years under the unmarked mound on which it once stood.

Had they known their dismal fate those young soldiers may

have objected, but that wasn't the Australian way, and despite the futility of their cause, they committed to what lay ahead and went down fighting.

Their 1st Division had begun the battle with a flourish by taking the village and refusing to give it up, but their holding out under the relentless German artillery attacks had cost them 5000 of their men. By the time the 2nd Division, with Lavarack in its lines, relieved them, those still alive from the 1st staggered from the near-annihilated town to warn them that it wasn't over – that although they had initially won the day, Pozieres would continue to be a case of give and take.

Lavarack would later vouch for that from firsthand experience, because by then, the Germans had recouped from the element of surprise, and now lying in wait, were in no mood to let any Australian off lightly. Particularly not the officers, for the Germans were to soon find out that shooting soldiers sporting peaked caps and insignias on their shoulders was the fastest way to cause confusion and win the day.

The tactic didn't augur well for Lavarack, who as a brigade major didn't believe in ducking for cover. He was just lucky that the two wounds he was to sustain would be superficial; one bullet grazing his hip, while the shrapnel that was to rip skin from his cheek would leave only a small scar which, for the rest of his life, would mark him as a warrior and make him all the more dashing.

His wounds, he would find out, were a small price to pay considering that he was to survive the Battle of Pozieres, when more than 6,000 of his fellow soldiers from the 2nd Division wouldn't. It was to be a devastating casualty count that would top 23,000 when added to that of Australia's1st and 4th Divisions, whose men were to fight at their side.

–oOo–

At first, when ordered to attack, the men of the 2nd Division held back waiting for a better moment to improve their chance of success. When they realised that there'd never be one, they settled on simply trying to survive and advanced with brave hearts, hoping to make the best of it.

"You and your men must capture Pozieres' heights," had been the order from British Command to Australia's 2nd Division Commander, Major General James Legge.

It seemed do-able at the time, because he and his men had been buoyed by their 1st Division's initial success at Pozieres, and were now full of the competitive *'if they can do it, so can we'* spirit. For that reason, they didn't expect their first attack to fail, but when it did and the Germans forced them back, it came as a blow to their pride, as did their alarming death toll.

Seeing those of his men who were still alive sitting despondent with their wounds, Legge knew exactly how to proceed.

"It s up you," he said to them. "Do you want to be withdrawn, or do we attack again?"

He knew deep down that they weren't defeated and wanted revenge; that despite their easy-going Australian natures, they were unrelenting when riled. Any enemy that thought they'd got the better of them had another thing coming.

That 'thing' was their second attack, which by way of blood, guts and determination, won them Pozieres' heights and saw them seize German positions there and beyond. Yet, It was a triumph that came at too high a price, for planting their flag at Pozieres lost Australia thousands of men, while by the end of the campaign, the Allies' total of dead and wounded was a startling 620,000 for advancing just seven miles.

CHAPTER 7

CONSIDERING THE 2ND DIVISION'S depleted numbers, it seemed an odd time to transfer Lavarack to the Australian 5th, but the Battle of the Somme was still in full swing and with its skyrocketing death toll and officers in such short supply, he was needed to command two of its artillery batteries.

It was only a pity, at this point, that he didn't have Blamey's insights into General Gough's dangerous ways, for with the battles of Bullecourt being in the man's incompetent hands, every Australian involved was on a one-way ticket to hell. They called it the Blood Tub, because it was best way to sum up its senseless slaughter. One which could have been avoided had Gough listened to advice.

"The new tanks you want for Bullecourt didn't perform well in their preliminary trials," Field Marshal Haig warned him, but rather than wait for the backup of more reliable artillery, Gough was set on being a trailblazer and insisted that the state-of-the-art machines should lead the way into combat.

"The Huns won't know what hit 'em!" he bragged with hands-on-hips bravado. "Our tanks will ram through their barbed wire and give Australia's 4th Division all the protection it needs."

His decision was fatal, for before the battle even began, half of his spanking new tanks broke down, while those that managed to move did so at a snail's pace before getting bogged in the mud.

The Australian troops they were meant to protect had no choice but to break out from behind, leaving themselves wide open to enemy fire. Yet, rather than run in retreat, they faced their fate head-on and charged towards the German line. Nothing, they thought, could make matters worse ... but they were wrong.

"We're on our own!" one of them called out to the others when he found out that they'd been issued hand grenades without detonators.

It meant that they were mincemeat under the German's machine-gun fire armed with only rifles. Hundreds of them went down, and seeing their fellow soldiers collapse like a pack of cards around them, those still alive fell back, stumbling across the blood-soaked ground, while having to side-step Gough's tanks sitting broken and burning on the battlefield.

Unable to stop the slaughter, their commander, Major General William Holmes, was beyond being diplomatic.

"Nearly four thousand of my men have been killed or wounded, and for what?" he stormed into Gough's headquarters to say.

But Gough replied without blinking:

"I'm sure your boys will do better next time round."

That second Battle of Bullecourt he had in mind was nearly a month away, and in the interim, conditions for those preparing for it were appalling. Only a day before he died, one soldier wrote home:

> *Why bother worrying about the enemy when the incompetence, callousness and personal vanity of our own commanders is killing us. We are lousy, stinking, ragged, unshaven, and go without sleep. I have one puttee, a dead man's helmet, another dead man's gas protector, and a dead man's bayonet. My tunic is rotten with other men's blood, and partly splattered with a comrade's brains. All here is horrible!*[8]

"We must see beyond their suffering," Gough said when the Australian commanders pleaded their men's cause. "I am determined to break the Hindenburg Line, and it's here, at Bullecourt, that we're going to do it."

Having decimated Australia's 4th Division, Gough set about achieving his goal by sending in its 2nd. They faltered at first under enemy fire, but then struck out again to take a large stretch of the German trenches. There, holding out against near overwhelming odds, until their 1st and 5th Divisions came to the rescue. As part of that relief column, Lavarack and his artillery batteries arrived just in time to see the worst of it.

"Howitzers to the left, and set up the heavy mortars over there!" he called out in command, having to point to the intended positions, because he could barely be heard above the bedlam going on around him.

His order was easier given than done when the horse-drawn carts carrying his artillery were close to immobile in the mud. After a month of torrential rain their wheels couldn't find traction in it, while having fought their hooves free from its suction, the horses in harness were rearing in terror, with their nostrils flared and wild, red eyes reflecting the fire and smoke swirling around them. Nothing could be done to rein them in until a random volley of enemy fire felled them.

Down went thousands of pounds of horseflesh, crushing men, both dead and alive, deep into the sludge to spare their Australian mates the bother of having to bury them.

Yet as the battle raged on, Gough remained undeterred.

If this is to be a victory solely for victory's sake, he decided, *then so be it and damn the consequences.* For thus far, in a campaign designed to be fought by just one Australian division, he had exhausted the resources of their 1st, 2nd and 4th, and was now relying on their 5th to save the day.

Its troops helped him out by holding the Germans at bay until more British troops arrived. Their linking up as one should have seen the enemy back off, but instead, it triggered fierce counterattacks that turned Bullecourt into the focus of an epic struggle.

One, which for the Australians under siege, came down to a matter of pride. In their dogged refusal to relinquish what they'd already captured of the Hindenburg Line, they buckled down to endure a seven-day enemy bombardment that shook the ground beneath them and shuddered through every sinew of their shell-shocked bodies.

At last the guns fell silent, and for the first time in what seemed like a century, Lavarack and his men got some sleep. When they woke the next morning, the sun had broken through the clouds and the Germans were gone.

"I knew that if we stuck it out we'd win!" Gough said to stake his claim on their success.

He expected praise and wondered why his Australian officers were looking at him with such disdain.

It was their way of saying that they'd never forgive him for orchestrating the unholy butchery that finally moved the Germans from Bullecourt's fields. By the time they left, those fields weren't worth having, for as far as the eye could see, there was nothing but slush, slaughter and bomb holes filled with the blood of the 10,000 Australians who'd been killed, wounded or gone missing.

Some would say that 'it was the stoutest achievement of the Australians in France'.[9]

Yet, with its litany of unforgivable errors and a death toll from which the AIF would never fully recover, it caused its troops dismay, distrust and utter contempt for their British commanders.

"I'll always hold Haig and Gough responsible for that bloodbath," Lavarack heard a fellow officer say, and until the end of the war, and for the rest of his days, he'd feel the same.

CHAPTER 8

THE ALLIES, NONETHELESS, were going from strength to strength thanks largely to the Australian Corps. It was biggest on the Western Front, and under the command of Lieutenant General Monash, now had a string of wins under its belt and well-worn boots.

The dusty pair that had seen Lavarack through Bullecourt was now helping him set a sturdy pace down the road to Amiens. After his 5th Division's victories at the Battles of Dernancourt and Villers-Bretonneux, he'd been transferred to Australia's 4th, and now as a Lieutenant Colonel, was under orders to push forward with his troops and hold the front line.

Unfortunately, the rest of the Allied forces were going in the other direction. All of them bedraggled and battle-weary and moving as fast as their tired legs could take them from the might of the renewed German thrust.

"You're going the wrong way!" Lavarack called out as the commander of a British siege artillery brigade sped past in his armoured car. Not fast enough, however, to miss what Lavarack said and have his driver slam on the brakes.

"You Australians think you can do anything!" he strode over from his car to say. "But you haven't a chance of holding them."

The contempt in his tone was meant to put the colonial in his place, but rather than rise to the challenge, Lavarack calmly answered:

"Will you stay and support us if we try?"

At that pivotal moment all animosity was gone, and looking hard at Lavarack to get his measure, the British brigadier replied:

"Right you are."

It was the best call he could have made, because the Battle of Amiens, for the Allies, was a decisive win. It cost them 19,000 men, but with the enemy suffering a death toll of thousands more, those of senior rank among the Germans realised that they had lost the war.

Men like Lavarack had made it happen, and as a result, his reputation as a cool-headed commander was growing. So much so, that Monash, himself, suggested that he be transferred to his Australian Corps' 1st Division.

As its GSO1, Blamey wasn't all that happy about sending the order, because he'd never liked Lavarack and sensed he was trouble. Despite being the only two Australians who'd earlier worked together at the British War Office, they'd never really meshed and Blamey was sure that, somewhere down the track, their strong personalities were bound to clash.

He didn't have long to wait before that track took a turn in Lavarack's favour.

Blamey, to this point, had been the star among staff officers after having planned the attack that took Pozieres. He had been dining out on its success ever since, but the Allies' subsequent and spectacular victory at the Battle of Hamel meant that he now had to share the limelight with Lavarack, who as his GSO2, had played a big part in masterminding the show.

As an exceptional man himself, Blamey wasn't prepared to pass the baton to another man said to be the same, and for the first time, he felt the pinch of Lavarack stepping on his toes. Luckily, Lavarack was his subordinate and easy to keep in check, but bit by bit, he was encroaching on his space and it was getting harder for Blamey to compete when whatever he did, Lavarack did better.

If discussing literature or religion, Lavarack could quote from any source, and if need be, do it in Latin. When it came to sport, he could present a cabinet full of trophies that said he was a champion. Where Blamey could speak three languages, Lavarack was fluent in four; and when the talk turned to military tactics, Lavarack knew exactly how to reconnoitre. Such a host of attributes should have put other men's noses out of joint, but with his charm and ready wit, Lavarack made it impossible for anyone to dislike him.

Blamey, however, was beginning to do so with an intensity that would ramp up over the years, and for the rest of their lives, stymie Lavarack's career. No matter how long those lives of theirs lasted, Blamey was determined to keep the upper hand. So he was alarmed when that strong hand of his suddenly started to shake and sweat as he succumbed to a virus that swept him off his feet and back to London where he was bedridden for two months.

–oOo–

"You'll be 1st Division's Acting GS01 until Blamey returns to duty." Lavarack was informed.

It was good news for Lavarack, but it made Blamey bend over and retch into a bucket. Apart from his violent vomiting and raging temperatures, he was spitting chips about Lavarack being given his chance to excel. Yet it worked like a miracle cure, because Blamey knew that if he didn't get back on his feet fast, he might lose his footing forever.

Monash would have told Blamey not to worry for he still saw him as being the best in staff officer material, and didn't stint in saying as much in his dispatch to the War Office:

> *No reference to the staff work of the Australian Corps can be complete without a tribute to the work and personality of my Chief of Staff, Brigadier General T. A. Blamey. With a mind widely informed and cultured far above the average, he serves me with an exemplary loyalty for which I owe a debt of gratitude that cannot be repaid.*[10]

After seeing what Monash had written, Blamey thought he had it in the bag, but with Lavarack's capable hand and equally brilliant mind in the mix, he wasn't to rest on his laurels for long; only for a few months, in fact, when on November 11, 1918, peace was declared and a select group of senior Allied officers gathered together to celebrate winning The Great War.

Blamey was seated next to Monash at the banquet table, but when dinner was done, he got up to do the rounds of the room. By the time he returned, Lavarack was in his chair and had Monash's undivided attention.

Contrary to what Blamey believed, their talk had nothing to do with the military, but with their shared passion for classical music. It was tempting to butt in, but Blamey thought better of it, deciding instead to stand silently seething for what seemed like the interminable amount of time that they sat with their heads together, oblivious to everyone else in the room.

Yet, when the evening was over and Monash stood up to leave, he showed no sign of having bonded with Lavarack beyond shaking his hand. That was heartening, and would have been enough for Blamey to breathe a sigh of relief had Monash not said to him in confidence as he left:

"That chap, Lavarack ... he's one to watch."

And Blamey agreed, because from that point on, he would watch every move he made, but not in the way Monash meant.

CHAPTER 9

DESPITE HIS NEW-FOUND ENTHUSIASM for Lavarack, however, Monash was still betting on Blamey being the best man to handle Australia's military future, but he may have changed his mind had he lived long enough to see how he performed in WWII. That Second World War, though, was still 21 years away and, in the meantime, both Blamey and Lavarack were busy building their careers.

They had arrived back in Australia after a seven-year absence, and at the prospect of a lasting world peace, were finally able to get back to business and devote themselves to their families. Blamey, by now, had two sons to carry on his name, while Lavarack, as was the way of it, had three.

When it came to their work, however, Blamey had the edge. While Lavarack took up a good post at the Royal Military College, Duntroon, Blamey, with his inimitable way of winning friends and influencing people, was made Deputy Chief of the General Staff with a mandate, in 1921, to create an Australian Air Force. He was ever a man of initiative and got straight on with the job, promptly taking possession of all existing aircraft at Melbourne's Point Cook and calling this new rough and ready flying fleet of his, the RAAF.

There was no time to concern himself with anything less important, so Lavarack's career, being at this point eclipsed by his own, slipped down Blamey's list of priorities. He was barely aware that Lavarack had quickly been promoted to Duntroon's 2nd in command, and as such, was drilling into a new generation of military officers mindsets that matched his own.

Within a year, he had done such a good job of it that he was moved to Melbourne Army HQ and into to the key post as Director of Military Training, which made him responsible for the entire Australian Army. Warning lights began to flash and Blamey was back on the alert, because his own career had suddenly hit a snag.

It had been flattering at first when he was asked to go to London as the Australian representative on the Imperial General Staff, but when he arrived, he was made to feel redundant. In the communiqué he sent home, he sounded decidedly surly:

> *It appears that the concept of an Imperial General Staff is absolutely dead!.The British Army sees little use for a combined staff coordinating the defense of the British Empire.*

He hadn't taken long to realise that he'd been invited purely as window dressing, and feeling somewhat reduced, he was sure that the British saw him as being of little consequence and no more than a diplomatic inconvenience.

Yet still, he kept striving to impress them; going so far, against his better judgment, as to back their short-sighted

Singapore Strategy, which was supposed to safeguard Britain's southern colonies in the event that a world conflict should happen again. With Japan's recent warmongering in South East Asia, the chance of it happening looked likely, but Britain's plan came nowhere near solving the problem.

"Our best defence against mounting Japanese aggression is to set up a Royal Naval base in Singapore," the British military hierarchy proposed.

Blamey raised his hand in favour, which was a weak gesture that he instantly regretted, given that it spelt disaster for his own country. Though well-intentioned and seeming to make sense, the policy failed to factor in other contingencies that could come up – that while Japan was dreaming of world domination, a new rabble-rouser in Germany would be working to achieve the same, switching Britain's focus back to Europe and keeping its ships so busy in the Atlantic that there'd be few left to send south.

None of it augured well for Australia which, until this point, had been so safe sitting happily down south. But now, with its barely tapped abundance of fertile land and unlimited, raw resources, it was soon to become the natural-product-poor, over-populated Japan's prime target.

So far, Hitler hadn't thrown his hat into the ring, but even without him in the picture, Blamey was sure that Britain's strategy wouldn't save his nation if it were put under threat. He continued, however, to back it. Initially, because he didn't want to rub his English peers the wrong way; and then later, purely to spite Lavarack, who was to stand alone, risking the wrath of all around him, to bravely oppose it.

Unfortunately, the Singapore Strategy was destined to be set in stone, and in reward for having been so strongly in support of it, Blamey was put forward as the Chief of the Australian

General Staff by the people in power who shared his unerring faith in the Mother Country.

"But that's outrageous!" other more senior officers who were waiting in line and weren't so fond of him complained.

The most vocal of them was Major General Victor Sellheim, who as Quartermaster General and a soldier who served with distinction in both the Boer and Great War, thought it a disgrace that he'd been pushed aside in preference for Blamey, who relatively speaking, was the new boy on the block.

To smooth his ruffled feathers, Lieutenant General Sir Harry Chauvel, to whom no-one objected, was given the role, while in an unprecedented move Blamey was placated with the title of Second CGS, just in case he was disappointed.

"Why the need to mollify him?" the other top-ranking officers who'd been overlooked were left to wonder, when they were expected to simply grin and bear it.

What should have been a win for Blamey, however, turned out to be a bit of a dead end.

"I'm going to throw in the towel," he told his wife after three years in the job, because he was bored and could see no immediate prospects of further advancement.

Though surprised, she knew better than to question her husband's decisions, and when he left for work the next day, she waved him off at the front gate with a smile.

The official document of transfer from the Permanent Military Forces to the Militia was on his desk by noon. It meant that he would be merely a part-time soldier for the next 14 years, but Blamey signed off on it, because he was tired of wearing khaki and was wondering what he'd look like in blue.

PART TWO

BLAMEY IN BLUE

CHAPTER 10

"WE NEED SOMEONE STRONG to sort out this mess," Monash said when he was asked to set up a Royal Commission to investigate what was wrong with Victoria's Police Force.

What had begun with civilised requests by its constables for better pay and working conditions had erupted into a wildcat strike that had thrown Melbourne's streets into chaos. Shops were looted, windows were smashed, and while two upturned trams in the city square were set on fire, three men had been killed.

The crowds that gathered to watch were booing the men responsible, but didn't have a clue why those men were doing it. As with everything, it came down to money and the fact that the police weren't being paid enough of it while working long hours without the backup of an industry pension.

Constable William Brooks, as their spokesman, had given the Victorian Police Commissioner, Alexander Nicholson, fair warning:

"Our other Australian states have police force pension programs in place, and we're sick to death of your empty promises to give us the same."

Although he was standing before the Commissioner with hat in hand, neither this courtesy, nor the stiff collar he'd put on for the occasion, could hide his hostility and red-hot passion for the cause.

To counter it, Nicholson said in bland response: "I promise to look into the matter as soon as possible."

His words were enough to give Brooks a modicum of hope, but that was wishful thinking when Nicholson's idea of 'looking into the matter' was to hire spies within their own police ranks to monitor every move their cops-on-the-beat made.

"*Traitors!*" those men were called by their fellow workers parading outside police headquarters with painted placards that read:

All we want is enough pay
to provide for our families!

It would have been sensible, if not humane, to succumb to their demands, but the executives looking down on them from their top office went a different way. Deciding, as they smoked their cigars in their pin-stripe suits, to fire the 636 policemen crying poor, while making sure that they never worked for them again.

In one fell swoop, a third of the Victorian Police Force was gone, leaving a gaping hole in the state's law enforcement, along with an empty leather chair in the Chief Commissioner's office. For after all the stress, and having caused most of it himself, Nicholson suddenly resigned citing ill-health. It was no surprise and no one was sorry to see him go, because it left the way open for someone with more savvy to take over.

"Blamey's your man," Inspector General Chauvel said to Monash, as he took his seat at the Royal Commission table.

When his recommendation received a resounding 'Aye' from the rest of the board, Blamey was made Chief Commissioner for the next five years. There to run the show, for better or worse, and some would say, under very shady circumstances.

CHAPTER 11

THE CONSENSUS AMONG THOSE in high places, before long, was not to question Blamey's morality while he was doing such a good job. Despite many a raised eyebrow, they decided to ignore his bad habits behind the scenes, including his weakness for women working in rooms with red lights.

"Why complain?" they reasoned, when Blamey had fixed the Victorian Police problem almost as soon as he sat down in the Commissioner's chair.

Though hired to take a hard line, he had pursued a better course, for beyond his own social climbing, Blamey never forgot his own beginnings and, as a man of the people, was rarely unfair to them.

"I believe the men's cause is just, even though they went about it the wrong way," he said before taking immediate measures to improve their pay and conditions.

"And furthermore," he added as he stamped the official paperwork. "I'm doing a complete overhaul of the system by introducing a faster police promotion scheme based on merit."

It was a scheme that set high standards and raised morale but, strangely enough, wasn't popular with the Police Association and was squelched the second Blamey later moved back to the military. Yet, those of his many initiatives that were to stay in place injected new life into the force and kept it in stride with the times. Fresh ideas, such as introducing police dogs, providing patrol cars with two-way radios, and giving women more incentives to join the force.

It wasn't the women he put in police uniform, however, who had his undivided attention.

–oOo–

"Break down the door!" Detective Riley Scott ordered, when he and his four-man team raided the brothel in Melbourne's slum suburb of Fitzroy.

It wasn't the first time they'd done it, so they knew their way around and moved from room to room by rote with flashlights and whistles blaring. Amid the screams of indignant prostitutes and those of their customers caught stark naked, many were arrested before the squad reached the end of the corridor, where a closed door barred the way to what was called 'the prestige suite'.

"Put your shoulder into it!" Scott shouted, when the locked door refused to give way,

But with his sergeant's shoulder not proving strong enough, Scott put his own to the task and the door came crashing down.

The lights in the room were off, and with its curtains drawn, it was hard to see anything but the outline of a four-poster bed and the blurred shape of a man and woman lying in it. There was a moment of dead-quiet disorientation, but then the man under the sheets in the shadows spoke:

"It's all right boys," he said, calmly holding up what looked like a police badge in his hand.

It was difficult to discern in the dim surrounds, but Scott could clearly see its gold embossed No. 80 glinting through the dark.

"Now back out of the room my lads," the mystery man then ordered with surprising authority given the circumstances. "And get on with your work."

By the time they'd done what they were told and registered what had happened, Scott was sure that whoever it was had escaped out the back door. He was curious, however, and wasn't going to let the culprit off the hook.

"Who belongs to Badge 80?" he asked the police records clerk when he got back to base.

The answer stopped him dead in his tracks.

No one ever knew whether it was Scott or someone else, who put two and two together and told the newspaper reporter, but the next day, both the brothel's and Blamey's name were splashed all over the front page.

It was the biggest scandal of its day, but when Blamey was called to account by the police tribunal, he didn't miss a beat:

"It *was* my badge," he was happy to admit. "But it wasn't I who had it at the time."

The president of the tribunal looked at him aghast and answered:

"Well that's worse than the crime itself, when you're bound to your badge by oath and should have it on your person at all times."

"Of that, I am now most regrettably aware," Blamey answered. "I have no excuse but to call it my misplaced trust in an old friend and fellow soldier from the French trenches."

He was counting on the fact that The Great War still evoked emotion and that those who fought in it deserved a little leeway.

Having reminded the tribunal of as much, he tried to wrap up his argument as quickly as possible:

"We all know that our restrictive liquor laws often make it hard for the men who most need it to get a stiff drink. I was merely helping out an old mate still suffering from shell shock by giving him the key to my locker at the Naval and Military Club, which I'm sorry to say, had some whiskey hidden in it."

Most men, including those on the tribunal, were guilty of stashing the same and thought that, on this issue, it was better not to pursue the matter. They still couldn't see, however, what the key had to do with his badge.

They were about to ask when Blamey beat them to it:

"My badge..." he said,"... was on the same keyring."

It sounded like the truth, but the fact that he had been so careless left the president of the tribunal no option but to offer Blamey an out before more damage was done.

"You must give us the man's name in order to clear your own."

Here, however, Blamey held up his hand to call a halt on proceedings.

"That sir, I refuse to do," he stated. "So deal with me as you must. Demote me or throw me into prison, but I will never give you his name, because his wife and children will suffer as a result."

It was an act of decency on Blamey's part that flew in face of all accusations that he was entirely without it. Somehow, and most skilfully, he had turned the tables. Yet, when the tribunal took a recess, Blamey knew its members weren't wholly convinced and that he had to get some help.

–oOo–

"Back me up on this will you ol' boy," he asked of Captain Stanley Savige, who had stood unfailingly at his side throughout The Great War and ever since.

Right now, Blamey needed him there more than ever, because his innocence, as yet, wasn't beyond reasonable doubt and Savige was the best man to speak in his defence. As a recipient of the military cross and the man who would later play the major role in setting up Legacy Australia, Savige was above reproach and his word went without question.

In this instance, his words stated, unequivocally, that Blamey had his full support:

"It couldn't have been Police Commissioner Blamey who was seen at the brothel, because he was with me at the time," Stanley said with a certainly that settled the matter.

He had saved Blamey's skin, and for that, Blamey would one day repay him.

–oOo–

Now with the dirt swept under the rug, it would have been better for Blamey to leave well enough alone, but the fact that he got away with it made him all the more brazen. Particularly when it came to Victoria's strict limitations on liquor and the ways in which a man of the law could get around them.

"As policemen, we must enforce the 6 o'clock closing regulation for all our public houses," he announced to the press for the sake of good publicity and to keep up what he wanted the world to think was his own respectable reputation.

But, as adamant as he was that the general public should stick to the rules, he was surer still that they didn't apply to him. While many a pub was raided for abusing the restrictions, the one that Blamey frequented stayed open all hours, with its publican reassuring its patrons that they were at no risk if they lingered longer at the bar.

"Don't' worry. The police won't touch us," he said with a wink whenever Blamey was there drinking in the back room.

It was the go-ahead for them to do the same – to share many a happy hour as police cars, with blaring sirens, roared up and down the road, shutting down every other hotel showing signs of life.

"He's a good bloke behind his stern façade," many a man who drank with Blamey felt free to say, for his drinking habits were hardly a secret and there was a hint of humour in the whole situation. However, those who were being arrested for breaking the same law, didn't think it was funny at all.

CHAPTER 12

LAVARACK'S LIFE, by comparison, was a bit more boring, because he was going by way of the straight and narrow with his focus fixed on the military.

Having done another stint at London's Imperial Defence College, he had returned home in 1929 as a brevet colonel and was getting on with the serious business of saving Australia. To that end, while sailing back to its shores, he'd been in deep debate with his fellow student and countryman, Frederick Shedden, over the Australian Government's adoption of the Singapore Strategy.

He had his work cut out for him, because as a public servant, Shedden was by build short, natty and precise, and by nature – clever and absolutely implacable. He had been the first Australian civilian to attend the college, and having been extended that honour, was forever beholden to its commandant and to all else that was British.

Many Australians felt the same, resting safe in their belief that Britain's word was gold and that its plan to set up a naval base in Singapore as a precaution against another war was the perfect solution.

"It's not!" Lavarack argued. "If we rely entirely on the British Navy, it will be fatal. If it comes again to war, England will have to prioritise its own survival in the north and won't have the spare ships or time to even look south."

"I don't believe that England will ever let us down, no matter how dire the circumstances," Shedden fought back in blind faith. "And you mustn't forget that our own ships will be there to supplement whatever shortages there are in the British fleet."

"But that's the point," Lavarack shot back. "We're not a naval nation, so our scant ships won't make a scrap of difference. I say that we stick to our strengths and sink the bulk of our resources into building an army big and powerful enough to protect our own borders."

Everything he said made sense, but by the time he and Shedden arrived back in Melbourne, Lavarack felt as if he'd been banging his head against a brick wall, for Shedden hadn't taken his words to heart and seemed set on blocking his ears to them in the future.

It didn't help Lavarack's cause when, soon after, Shedden was appointed Secretary of the Defence Committee looking into the matter. That committee included the chiefs of staff of all three services, which meant that Lavarack had an uphill battle trying to present his case. Not that it mattered, when the committee's bandying words over the years achieved little more than giving Shedden the opportunity to improve his own political connections.

By 1932, Shedden was accompanying the Minister of External Affairs to the League of Nations' Disarmament Conference, and soon after, was appointed Australian Representative to the British Cabinet, where he befriended its Secretary, Sir Maurice Hankey.

And that was a relationship well worth cultivating, but Shedden did it with such verve that it turned into hero worship, He, with his mouse-like build and constant mimicking of the man, making it impossible for the Fleet Street press to resist calling him 'the pocket Hankey'.

Lavarack cringed at the thought of being labeled anything of the like. Yet despite it being so demeaning, he could see that Shedden was shrewdly positioning himself in the power game and would soon be a man who was better to have onside than off. Unfortunately, for Lavarack, it would always be the latter.

Shedden made his opposition to him official in 1934 when Hankey, with whom he shared all opinions, came to Australia to discuss the state of military affairs. As Secretary of the Committee of Imperial Defences, Hankey had his finger on the pulse and nothing – most definitely not Lavarack's point of view – was going to shift his summation of the situation:

> *Even in the very extreme case of simultaneous trouble in Europe and the Far East, Britain would have the numerically superior battle fleet to ensure a marginal advantage in both theatres.*[11]

"What a load of bunkum!" Lavarack said out loud when he finished reading Hankey's report.

He felt safe saying as much sitting alone in his office, but he wouldn't have hesitated saying it again to others or putting it in writing, because he was sure that, despite all his glib assurances, Hankey knew perfectly well that splitting the fleet between Europe and the Far East would compromise both battle zones. In fact, his deliberate skirting of the truth made it clear that, in an emergency, a British naval force of any effective size wouldn't be sent at all.

Fortunately, Lavarack was now Chief of the General Staff and Head of the Australian Army, and as such was expected to submit his opinion of Hankey's appraisal. It was finally his time to have his say and he wasn't going to hang back, for when it came to Australia's dangerous over-reliance on the Royal Navy and its neglect of its own land forces, he didn't care whether he rubbed Hankey, Shedden or both the British and Australian governments the wrong way.

It meant that he had to get into the ring to fight it out, pulling no punches until he stoked Shedden's open hostility and caused considerable friction with the Australian Government and its successive Ministers of Defence. Yet undaunted, he threw his first blow by reading out his response to Hankey's recommendations:

> *Whilst Sir Maurice Hankey's advice should receive the respect and attention due to his high authority, it should not be allowed to obscure consideration of what is a purely Australian problem. I fear that in his favouring of the navy, he underestimates the value of land and air forces, and I think it far better that the defence vote should be distributed more evenly between them.*

He paused here to let his words sink in, and then forged ahead amid the uneasy murmurs of those in attendance at the 1937 Imperial Conference.

> *To safeguard Australia, I recommend the following: That no further commitment to the Singapore Strategy be taken until the British Government has guaranteed the completion date of its base in Singapore; that they tell us the strength of the naval forces to be dispatched there in an emergency; and that they let us know how long it will take them to get there.*[12]

It was a blatant attempt to pin Britain down, and its politicians didn't like it. They didn't appreciate being called out on their empty promises, and for that matter, nor did the Australians who were forever in support of them. One, was Australia's Minister for Defence, Sir Archdale Parkhill, who having been swayed by Hankey's and Shedden's views, stood up and said in swift retort:

"The observations made by Major General Lavarack involve implications of a highly political nature. In this, he has overstepped his bounds and should limit his remarks to only the technical aspects of the scheme."[13]

"I can assure you, sir, that my observations are based purely on strategic consideration," Lavarack countered. "And in making them I did not mean to trespass on political territory."

It was obvious, however, that he'd done just that, not by mistake, but intent, and Britain's Naval Secretary wasn't pleased.[14]

When he glared at Lavarack with a look that could kill, words weren't necessary.

"How dare you!" his expression said instead. *"Who are you to suggest that the privileges of what has always been our supreme Royal Navy should run in parity with the air force and army?"*

But Lavarack had said what he had to say, risking the enmity of the Empire for the sake of Australia.

CHAPTER 13

BLAMEY WOULD HAVE BEEN IN on the argument with all guns blazing had he not still been in the Police Force. His days within its ranks, however, were numbered and most were saying that the sooner he left the better.

Although his career there had been successful in many ways, it was steeped in controversy and he had just crossed the line for the last time by attempting to cover up the shooting of the Superintendent of the Criminal Investigation Branch, John Brophy.

Blamey had appointed him to the post, but because the attack was during business hours and Brophy had someone else's wife in the car with him, he was now in need of protection against the seedy implications. The woman's jealous husband had most likely fired the shots, but to protect both Brophy's and her reputations, Blamey stated under oath:

"Superintendent Brophy was rendezvousing with a police informer in regard to one of his investigations. When he realised it was a set up, he most commendably fired at the armed bandits, but accidentally shot himself."

"What three times!" Victoria's Premier, Albert Dunstan exclaimed, scoffing at the absurdity of the testimony before he gave Blamey the choice to either resign or be dismissed.

Dismissal meant the loss of his pension and any future prospects of being employed by the public service or army, so Blamey signed his letter of resignation and strode out the door. Though scowling as he went, breathing a sigh of relief, because he'd pretty much got off scot-free.

Nevertheless, he went straight to the corner pub to drown his sorrows.

"Everything in my life is on a downhill slide," he confided to the publican over a pint of beer.

It wasn't like him to wallow in self-pity, but over the last two years what had been his unconquerable spirit felt spent for having suffered the loss of his long-invalided wife, Minnie, and the recent shock death of his eldest son, Charles, who he'd fondly called Dolf.

It was a bad omen, Blamey's superstition now told him, to have named his son after a friend who'd been killed in a freak shooting accident when young. In doing so, he'd as much as condemned Dolf to die in a similar, unexpected way.

The phone call that came to say that his son, Flight Officer Charles Blamey, had been fatally injured in a plane crash at the RAAF's Richmond training base, would be forever emblazoned on his brain, while thoughts of his boy's body burning in the flames, would haunt him for the rest of his life and have him wake each night in fright.

With one son down before his flying career even got off the ground, Blamey couldn't bear the loss of another. The onus was now on his second son, Thomas, to carry on the family name, and Blamey swore that, from this point on, he'd protect him by any means possible.

It had been a terrible two years, and being knighted in the middle of them presented Blamey with such a mixed bag of emotions that he didn't know whether to rejoice or resort to tears. The publican's advice from across the bar was to follow his heart and go where he felt he was most needed. And that, to Blamey, meant returning to the army, where despite his past litany of indiscretions, he was welcomed with open arms.

In many ways he'd never left its ranks, for during the Depression, he had supplemented his Police Commissioner's income by making broadcasts on Melbourne radio. Their main thrust was to alert the Australian public to the state of international affairs, which he was sure were soon to have a devastating impact on them.

"I'm swimming in dangerous waters, so I'll go by the alias of 'The Sentinel'," he told the program's producer, for like Lavarack, much as he hated to admit it, Blamey was standing guard over his country and had its best interests at heart.

"I am appalled by Hitler's persecution of Jews!" he said over the wireless, long before most people realised the full fear factor of Germany's new Fuhrer. "There is definitely a clear and growing menace to world peace from both that nation and the Empire of Japan."

He called it the way it was, and with his colourful, contentious talks doing wonders for the radio station's ratings, they were to continue until just days before the World War of which he warned began.

CHAPTER 14

IT WAS A WORRYING PROSPECT, but despite being in anticipation of it, Blamey had found time, in between broadcasts, to marry again. This time, putting a ring on the finger of fashion artist, Olga Farnsworth, who though twenty years his junior, equaled him in every way and would be his mainstay for the rest of his life.

As the wife of who was now Sir Thomas Blamey, she was a lady in every sense, and throughout the Second World War, would go wherever she was needed; not only matching her husband in resilience, but outstripping him by a country mile when it came to showing compassion for the troops.

"I'll do whatever it takes for our boys," she said when she joined the Red Cross.

That commitment was to take her to frontline field hospitals where she tended to the wounded, while her work would carry on long after the war in caring for the emaciated POWs, who somehow survived Changi Prison. For that, those men who took months to recover, would forever thank her, while the

Australian Government would do the same by awarding her the Order of the British Empire.

Their honeymoon, in the meantime, had been a rushed affair. With World War II imminent, whatever romance there was between them played second fiddle to Blamey's new role as Controller General of Recruiting. A position of prime importance that came with a big, new desk and a set of job specs that read:

Expand the Australian Army ... and fast!

Blamey got straight on to the task and, in a remarkably short time, with his usual efficiency, managed to double the size of the part-time militia to 70,000. It was such a good result that, in March 1939, senior politicians, Henry Gullett and Richard Casey went to confer with the Australian Prime Minister.

"In the event of war, we want to put Blamey's name forward as Australia's Commander-in-Chief," they said to the aging and seriously ill, Joseph Lyons.

As a right-minded man, Lyons showed some hesitation, for while he respected both men and their opinions, he couldn't say as much for Blamey.

"I have serious concerns about the man's morals," he answered.

"Those concerns may well be valid," Casey was quick to reply. "But we both served with him at Gallipoli and in France, and from first-hand experience, know that there is no better man for the job."

Lyons still looked unconvinced, so Gullett gave it his last shot:

"We've got some brilliant staff officers, sir," he said. "But Blamey is a commander, and that's the difference."

His words were enough to have Lyons summon Blamey to a meeting in Canberra, where against his better judgment, he had to agree that there was something compelling about his presence – a strength in his now portly stance and firm manner that put others, including better men, in their place. He was clearly one who wasn't afraid to speak his mind, yet at the same time, seemed to have the sense to keep his mouth shut and to sway whichever way was to his advantage. By the end of the interview Lyons was won over.

"He really is somebody!" he said to his fellow politicians, and because the Government was in search of a strong, yet politically pliable commander, Blamey's lesser side was overlooked and he was designated for the post.

He had hit the jackpot, but soon after suffered a moment of concern when Lyons suddenly died of a heart attack. Blamey only hoped that the late Prime Minister had put all the appropriate paperwork in place before he passed; but he had no need to worry, for Lyons was succeeded by Blamey's new friend, Robert Menzies. A man of solid Scottish descent, who had made up his mind to stay in the top job for a long, long time, and now, as one of Blamey's greatest fans, had no problem sticking to the plan.

"I've always admired the man," he said of Blamey when other names for the most senior military position were put forward.

Two of them were Major Generals Gordon Bennett and John Lavarack, who like Blamey had strong and well-connected supporters, but Menzies wasn't one of them.

"I'm not questioning their credentials," he said. "But both men, particularly Lavarack, are public critics of the Government's defence policies and that won't do."

On this matter, Menzies was immovable, for as an ambitious man and the most dedicated of Anglophiles, he didn't want anyone getting in his or England's way.

PART THREE

BLAMEY BACK IN ARMY BOOTS

CHAPTER 15

"YOU MUST TRUST ME ON THIS!" Lavarack said to the Council of Defence in what was now his heated frustration. "If it comes to war, Japan won't hesitate to take risks and will target Australia."

He had been saying the same since 1938, but now that Blamey was back in army boots and weighing in on every debate, Lavarack felt that he was fighting a losing battle.

A fact that was about to become more evident with Blamey having just got to his feet to make his usual confident rebuttal:

"Contrary to Major General Lavarack's beliefs, I am full of praise for our Government and the efficiency of its plans," he said in regard to the controversial Singapore Strategy.

It was only controversial because Lavarack and a few other men like him continued to question its good sense. In this, they were in the minority, and had to wait to say more, because Blamey still had the floor.

"In fact, it is reasonable to assume," he added, "that an invasion is unlikely."

His words of reassurance received a round of applause from the politicians who preferred what he said to Lavarack's dire words of warning.

This was Blamey at his best, always knowing how to win a crowd, even when putting forward views he didn't believe himself.

The man's a miracle, Lavarack had to concede, for despite being over 50, Blamey was still fit for the fight, expending his remarkable energy on battling him, rather than reserving his strength for those who would soon be his real enemies.

Their crossing of swords on the subject of Singapore had been going on for months. Yet still now, in March 1939, neither would let go of the bone, and Lavarack had just leapt from his seat in response to Blamey's reckless words:

"Can anyone here, show me that Singapore will be impregnable or will be made so?" he demanded of those in the conference room. "If Singapore proves vulnerable, and we are relying upon it to keep the enemy at a distance, then we are certainly living in a fool's paradise."[15]

A deathly hush fell over the room, and while those around him wondered whether to take exception, Lavarack used the silence as his window of opportunity and continued:

"I have no doubt that Japan, at this very moment, is waiting to launch either a series of raids or a full-scale invasion of Australia. We must look to no one but ourselves for protection by making sure that our Australian militia is strong and ready for war. Because believe me, when push comes to shove, Singapore will be out of the equation."

It all seemed so logical to Lavarack, and with such danger looming on their doorstep, he resented that his words still weren't being taken seriously. What angered him more, however, was knowing that Blamey secretly agreed with him, but was doggedly disputing everything he said simply on principle and to secure the popular vote.

"The problem with Lavarack is that he's too passionate," Blamey said later when it was certain that the Singapore Strategy was to stay in place. "He makes the mistake of caring too much about his cause."

Blamey was speaking from experience, for he'd mastered the art of staying detached, and had long since seen it as the best way to manipulate people. One of them was Defence Secretary Shedden, who would soon make his preference clear by ensuring that Lavarack, as the apostle of national defence, was overlooked in favour of Blamey for the command of the newly formed 2nd AIF.

It was a brave decision considering that Blamey had little experience as a combat commander and had spent most of WWI as a staff officer. But Shedden, apart from disliking Lavarack, was working on the wild assumption that some of the brilliance of John Monash, under whom Blamey served, had rubbed off.

CHAPTER 16

HITLER MARCHED HIS TROOPS into Poland in September 1939, and as soon as England and France said: '*This means war!*', Australia set up its Second Imperial Force, starting with its 6th Division.

Lieutenant General Blamey was put in command, while Lavarack was compensated with the role of GOC Southern Command. It was a senior post that required his rank being lifted to lieutenant general in line with Blamey's, but within a week, much to Blamey's relief, that rank of Lavarack's was to be reduced again to Major General in Command of Australia's 7th Division.

The order for that second division to be formed came directly from the War Cabinet.

"Australia's 6th and 7th Divisions will be grouped together as 1 Corps with Lieutenant General Blamey in overall command."

Someone, therefore, had to take over Blamey's prior leadership of the 6th.

"We think that it should be Lieutenant General Lavarack," those who were making the decision said.

"No, it should not!" Blamey shot back with a look that really said: *'Over my dead body!'*

When he saw their surprise at his vehement response, Blamey explained:

"I am rejecting the suggestion, because I believe the man has certain defects of character which make him unsuited to succeed me. I am, however, happy to have him put in command of my 1 Corps' new 7th Division on the proviso that his rank drops again to Major General."

It was a slap in the face, but as a means to an end Lavarack had to grin and bear it, while Blamey sat back feeling satisfied that their ranks were no longer on a par and that Lavarack was back where he belonged – forever a rung below him.

There was always the chance, of course, that Lavarack might step up that rung again by distinguishing himself in battle, Ahead of him was a six-year field of opportunity to shine, so Blamey would be pleased when later in the war, Lavarack's 7th Division became known as 'the Silent Seventh' due to its achievements being less lauded than those of all other Australian Divisions.

It was a nickname true, but unfair, for it was to be the result of the 7th's real role in the fierce Syrian Campaign being censored. That, and the fact that Blamey, under the convenient cover of complying with wartime security, would help keep quiet the outstanding part Lavarack played in it.

No one would ever know what caused the hostility between them, nor to which 'defects of character" Blamey referred. Certainly, under the extreme circumstances of a world war when good men were in high demand, Blamey could hardly say:

"It's just because I don't like him."

He believed he had good reasons for that, but the best of

them harked back to the scandal of his Police Commissioner days and the endless speculation about his missing badge.

"It was stolen," Blamey had taken to using as his excuse, because his initial explanation of having lent it to a friend hadn't gone down well with the tribunal and had made him feel like a fool.

Theft was far more acceptable and most with whom he'd mingled ever since seemed happy to nod their acceptance. All bar Lavarack, who when the subject was last publicly discussed calmly said:

"Or perhaps the reason why Blamey's badge was found in a brothel was because ... Blamey was in a brothel."

Those who heard him say it were tempted to laugh out loud, but just one look at Blamey's stone-cold expression had them keep their mouths shut.

It would have meant the end of all civility between them had this not been the one thing Blamey actually liked about Lavarack – that he never bad-mouthed him behind his back and always said what he had to say straight to his face.

Now, however, it was time to put their bickering aside and get down to the business of war.

CHAPTER 17

AUSTRALIA'S COMMITMENT to the Second World War would be remarkable with 15 per cent of its entire population mobilised and nearly one million serving in its armed forces.[16] Considering the country's relatively small population, and how much of it had been sacrificed to WWI, it was a wonder its soldiers weren't more gun-shy. Yet, once again, the nation's young men lined up in their uniformed legions and marched off to war.

They didn't know how many of them wouldn't come back: That 39,000 from their ranks would die, that 23,000 would be wounded; and that 30,000 would be taken prisoner.

Nor did they realise that those held captive in German stalags would be considered lucky, because the 22,000 who were to be taken by the Japanese would suffer such brutality and deprivation that only half their number would survive.

Already, the Royal Australian Navy and Air Force, respectively, were fighting with the British fleet or dying in dogfights over Britain, but it wasn't until January, 1940, that the Australian Army boarded the ships bound for the Middle East and Mediterranean.

Those ships were packed to the brim with the 6th, 7th and now 9th Divisions, who together with the troops from New Zealand, were flying the Anzac Corps flag. They were soon to set foot on the same hot sands as their WWI fathers – this time, not having to suffer the shock that had been Gallipoli, but to kick off their campaign with a rousing victory at the Battle of Bardia.

It took the 6th Division two days of intense fighting to take the Italian fortress town on the Libyan coast. There were cheers all round, for it was the first time in the war that the Australian Army fought a battle planned by Australians, under the command of an Australian general.

That command had gone to Major General Iven Mackay, who'd initially been earmarked to lead the 7th back when Lavarack was expected to take over the 6th.

–oOo–

"I want that switched around, with Lavarack to command the 7th and Mackay the 6th," Blamey had insisted, because with the 6th seeing action first, he wasn't going to let Lavarack get the kudos that went with it.

One way or the other, the 6th did a fine job, not only inflicting 41,000 Italian casualties, but taking the town and 40,000 prisoners. Most of those captured Italian soldiers, having lost their weapons during their rushed retreat from Egypt, poured from their posts with no guns and their hands held high.

"We surrender!" they called out to the Australians. "Now feed us!"

It was an enormous embarrassment for Mussolini and his military, but strangely enough, it was an Australian who seemed more upset.

"Is everything okay mate?" a supply truck driver stopped to say to the sole sergeant, who was looking so glum herding the horde of Italian prisoners down the road.

The soldier in his slouch hat stopped to take a cigarette from his pocket, and asking a prisoner to hold his rifle while he lit it, replied:

"You'd reckon they'd give me a fair crack of the whip. I joined the damn army to get away from my damn boring job in Australia, and here I am ..., damn well droving again!"

In military terms, however, it was a happy day and a victory worth celebrating given that it came at the fairly small cost of 130 Australian lives. Disregarding the other 350 who were wounded, it was a casualty count that could easily be written off in the army annals, but not by the 130 bereft families back home.

It was Mrs Lucy Stewart from Sydney who had the honour of being told that her husband was the first Australian Army officer to die in combat: That Captain Wilson, "Bill" Stewart had struck out bravely to set the start line for the assault on Bardia, but had been shot multiple times in the chest and was dead before his body hit the ground.[17]

The telegram had been worded in this way to assure her that her husband didn't suffer. It was only a shame that the same couldn't be said for the young wife and 4-year-old son he left behind.

–oOo–

Now that the 6th had done its duty in disposing of so many Italians, the British Commander-in-Chief of the Middle East, General Archibald Wavell, decided it was the 7th's turn to do the same to the Germans. This, however, lifted the game to a whole new level, for those thousands of Germans were kicking off their Balkans Campaign by invading Yugoslavia and Greece, and being more dedicated to destruction, were storming their way towards Athens.

For the Australians, the battle was lost before it even began, because there wasn't a hope that just one of their divisions could stop the deluge of enemy troops bearing down on them. Yet, for the sake of the Allied Cause, the British War Cabinet felt that it was worth the men of the 7th laying down their lives if only to briefly stall them.

It was clear that they were being sent to the slaughter, but it was for entirely different reasons that Blamey wouldn't have a bar of it.

"Absolutely not!" he stated when General Wavell said that Lavarack and his 7th Division should lead the charge. "I insist that the 6th strikes out first, because they're more battle-ready and up to the task of taking on the Wehrmacht."

The argument over which of the divisions deserved the right to be sacrificed went on for several days, but with Blamey being Blamey it was finally Wavell who backed down and bowed to his subordinate's wishes.

"All right," he said. "The 6th it is for Greece."

Lavarack was disappointed, but it was a blessing in disguise, because the whole campaign was destined to be relegated to the back pages of history under the heading of 'Abject Failure'.

It seemed to be a big win for Blamey on his 6th Division's behalf, but it was one for which its men wouldn't thank him. For they knew that his favouring them to go up against such impossible odds had nothing to do with them being the best, but was all about Blamey depriving Lavarack of the prize.

CHAPTER 18

LAVARACK WAS IN ALEXANDRIA loading his 7th Division onto ships when he received Wavell's change of orders:

Stop your embarkation for Greece and take your 18th Brigade to the Western Desert instead.

He thought he'd been side-lined, but he really should have been flattered, for he had been chosen to go to Tobruk to take on the Third Reich's finest.

"The best we can do to stop General Rommel and his Afrika Korp's rapid advance on Alexandria is to send in the Australians," Wavell had said at the military conference in Cairo. "If Lavarack's troops can take and hold the port of Tobruk, it'll not only stake our claim on all vital supply lines, but will rob Rommel of the same and stop his Panzer tanks in their tracks."

It was the perfect plan for what was revving up to be the

most violent, hard-fought campaign. With Lavarack in overall control, it was Australia's 9th Division, under the command of General Leslie Morshead, that was to take on the task, aided by four regiments of British artillery, the 3rd Indian Motor, and the 18th Brigade from Lavarack's 7th.

"The onus is on you and Morshead to come up with the most effective defence strategy," Wavell said, as he and Lavarack drove by jeep to Tobruk.

It was a burden Wavell felt confident in putting on their shoulders because, bit by bit, he was learning how Australian generals worked: That beyond winning, they cared about the welfare of their own, and even the enemy's men.

> *We must never forget that many soldiers fight valiantly and will die inside the blue lines officers draw on maps, Although we are here to fight and win, we must do it at the smallest possible cost.*

Wavell liked those words and had committed them to heart. He couldn't remember which man from the Australian military said them, but it didn't matter when it was an ethos that distinguished every one of its generals.[18] Sticking to that code of conduct had served them well throughout WWI, and if Wavell wanted them to carry on doing the same in WWII, he knew it was best to leave them to their own devices.

To this end, he believed that Lavarack should be put in command of the entire Western Desert Force, but Blamey came back with an emphatic 'no'.

"That won't happen!" he said with his trademark tenacity. "I've said it before, and I'll say it again – Lavarack is not suitable for such high command."

For the life of him, Wavell couldn't work out why when Lavarack struck him as being supremely capable. He could only conclude that that was the point – that for private, possibly competitive reasons, Blamey was keeping Lavarack's ambitions at bay, which seemed a shame when his services in a more senior role could well have been of benefit to their Allied cause.

It was a tired old tale where Lavarack was concerned, but much as he resented Blamey holding back his career, he would continue throughout it to respect the chain of command and to obey Blamey's orders without complaint.

His attention, in the meantime, had turned to Tobruk, and having conferred with Morshead, he reported back on its status to Wavell.

"The morale of our men is high and Tobruk has enough supplies and surrounding defensive works to withstand a siege for at least four months."

That wouldn't be long enough, for the Siege of Tobruk was destined to last double that time, with Rommel's tanks and troops pummeling the port garrison into the ground for a solid eight months.

The Allied troops within it were to be up against a superior force and, by rights, should have surrendered, but there was one thing Rommel hadn't factored into the equation: That finally, he and his unstoppable Afrika Korps would be fighting an enemy every bit as resolute and resilient.

"Why don't the bastards just give up?" one German officer shouted to Rommel through the gun smoke and hot, wind-whipped sands. "They're outnumbered, surrounded and are nothing but rats in a trap."

It was a comment that got lost in translation between trenches, so embracing what was intended as an insult as their epithet, the Australian Rats of Tobruk held on ... and held on... and after 242 days of what seemed like Armageddon, finally won out.

For the first time, Rommel was forced to fall back, and filled with dismay at the Australians' skill, determination and unconventional tactics, had something to say:

> *I fear and respect the Australians more than any other force, for they are reckless, ruthless and revengeful. If I wanted to take Hell, I'd use them to do it, and their New Zealand compatriots to hold it.*[19]

It was a triumph and tribute that Lavarack wasn't to see or hear, for despite having set up the siege for success and bonding with both his and Morshead's men, he was transferred only days after the siege began.

> *You are to hand over control of Tobruk to General Morshead and return to your old command of the 7th Division in Egypt. You will wait there for further orders.*

Blamey had sent these instructions a short time before he, himself, set out to supervise the Battle Of Greece. Having thought long and hard about issuing them, he'd reasoned it was the sensible thing to do to stop Lavarack covering himself with glory at Tobruk while he was gone.

Lavarack was more angry than surprised when he read them, because he'd done nothing wrong. The trouble was that he'd done too much right.

CHAPTER 19

BLAMEY, ALONG WITH Major General Mackay's 6th Division, arrived in Greece just days before it was invaded. For the first time since Gallipoli, Australia and New Zealand were flying the Anzac Corps flag, and with a lot to live up to would have done their forefathers proud had they been given even a ghost of a chance.

More than a million German and Italian troops were descending, via Yugoslavia, onto ancient Greek land, and like a swarm of killer ants were destroying everything in their wake. Within 21 days, they would take Athens and then set their sights on Crete.

"It's up to us to stop them," Blamey told the 17,000 men of Mackay's sole 6th Division.

Those men were used to having the odds stacked against them, but as much as they took pride in tackling battles of David and Goliath proportion, they knew that this one, with its staggeringly disproportionate numbers, was beyond them. Blamey could see it in their eyes, so he said what he thought might reassure them.

"You must take heart, because 40,000 British servicemen and women will be here to help you."

That made a total of 57,000, which still barely represented five per cent of the enemy troops storming towards them.

"What a mug's game!" one soldier mumbled to another as he and the rest in the 6th's ranks braced themselves to rush headlong into a losing battle.

Their one hope was to stay alive long enough to go into full retreat. So until then, they'd give it their best shot, because showing their backs to the enemy never sat well with any Australian.

–oOo–

"I didn't count on having to fight the elements as well as the enemy," Mackay said to the commander of his 19th Brigade, Lieutenant Colonel Alan Vasey.

They were making their rounds of the camp they'd set up near the northern Greek village of Vevi, and when they stopped to speak to the sergeant on guard duty he summed up the situation:

"It's bleedin' freezing here sir," he said, in answer to Mackay saying good morning.

Mackay liked to give his men a little leeway in expressing their opinion and, in this instance, would have smiled in agreement had his own lips, in the bitter cold, not been frozen stiff and clamped so tight over his own chattering teeth.

It was hard for them to acclimatize when they were all dog-tired. Since they'd arrived from North Africa, none of them had had a wink of sleep with the pelting rains in Northern Greece having turned to snowstorms that kept them wide awake and shivering every night in their tents.

The joke was on them when Greece had, at first, welcomed

them so warmly with fair weather and women, fairer still, throwing kisses and flowers as they marched through Athen's streets like conquering heroes.

Since they'd trudged further north to stop the Germans crossing the Yugoslav border, however, both the temperature and their egos had plummeted, and now, huddled under the protection of mere canvas walls, they were cursing their home country's warmer climate for leaving them ill-equipped to cope with the higher hemisphere's icy mountain conditions.

"The craggy mountains and wintry terrain will work against Hitler's Panzers," they had been told, but it came as little comfort when the same was working every bit as hard against them.

–oOo–

It all seemed such unnecessary suffering when, right from the start, neither Blamey nor Australia's Prime Minister Menzies had the slightest illusions about their mission being a success. All Menzies could do to soften the blow was to dictate his country's terms when negotiating with Britain's Prime Minister Churchill before the campaign began:

"We want your guarantee that if things turn out like Gallipoli, the British Navy will provide full and immediate evacuation for our Australian troops."

"Of course," Churchill promised in order to rope them into the scheme for his lost-before-it-even-began Greek operation.

Menzies still wasn't convinced, and to make sure that his Australians weren't to be sacrificed simply to stall the inevitable German advance, he added a further stipulation:

"And that unlike what happened in WWI, Australia will be privy to all military plans, at the top level, at all times."

"That goes without saying," Churchill confirmed, being as he was a dab hand at fudging the truth if it suited his and Britain's purposes.

It was, however, assurance enough for Menzies to commit Australia to the campaign, which for the sake of recorded history, he did with a flourish and some noble words:

We will not leave Greece in the lurch.[20]

With that Blamey had set out on the warpath, but before he and his Australian 1 Corps had even set foot on Greek soil, he'd put in place, with a practical sense of pessimism, plans for their emergency evacuation.

CHAPTER 20

THE ORDERS CAME from the British Head of Commonwealth Forces, Lieutenant General Henry Wilson, and Blamey passed them on the commander of his 6th Division.

"You are to hold back the Germans until April 12," he told Major General Mackay.

It was a big call considering that their campaign, as part of Operation Lustre, would come down to nothing but a strategic three-week withdrawal. One through which Brigadier Vasey and his 19th Brigade were expected to slow the German stampede while making their own systematic retreat to southern ports. They were to do it with nerves of steel and military precision, making a series of leapfrog manoeuvres and last stands to protect their mates' backs until they could all quit Greece for good and leave its hell behind them.

Before that could happen, however, the focus was on the village of Vevi, where the men of the 2/3 Field Regiment were doing their best to stem the German tide. They were the first Australian artillery unit to fire on the enemy, and having anticipated the worst, were surprised to see some success when the Germans' preliminary probing attacks failed and their war machines didn't live up to their maximum killing potential.

"What are they doing?" Lieutenant Colonel Strutt[21] of the 2/3 said in disbelief when the Germans boldly stopped their trucks only a short distance away, in full sight of them.

There, looking far too sure of themselves and showing flagrant contempt for the smaller Australian regiment standing ready to confront them, they began to casually unload their troops.

Their winning streak had evidently gone to their heads, and with no one, so far, having successfully got in their way, they saw themselves as being invincible. With that in mind, they weren't worried, in the least, about taking Greece when it merely meant continuing their Blitzkrieg style of rapid mobile warfare that had shaken the rest of Europe. In this instance, however, they'd got too big for their boots and hadn't considered the incapacity of the primitive Greek roads to carry their huge army group of 27 divisions.

"So let's wipe the smiles off their faces," Strutt said, seeing this window of opportunity that had the Germans just as restricted as were they by the rugged terrain and the wet, below-zero cold. It was a freeze factor that was chilling soldiers from both sides to the bone and making an impassable mire of the roads on which the Reich and its tanks were relying.

For the Australians, it seemed surreal suddenly coming face-to-face with the enemy, but when Mackay's orders started flying over the wires, they snapped into action, firing off their first rounds that screamed through the air with such speed and precision that the Germans backtracked faster than they'd advanced. So fast, that they left their trucks sitting, as if stunned, in the centre of the road, bearing witness to the fact that:

"Those Australians can shoot!"[22]

It felt good for the men of the 2/3 to have taught the enemy a lesson, but all they had really done was poke the bear by shocking the Germans out of their complacency.

By the time, those men of the SS had regrouped and pulled themselves together, they were resolved to show the Allies no mercy.

–oOo–

"It's a damn shame when this is such a beautiful spot," Commander-in-Chief of the Greek Army, General Alexander Papagos said to his British counterpart, General Wilson, as they looked out over the peaceful valley of Florina with its wildflowers and winding road leading through the hills to the village of Vevi.

Soon the scene's bright country colours would give way to the cratered fields of a soot-black battlefield, while the surrounding mountains, with their ridges cutting so clean against the azure sky, were to be shrouded in a cloud of filthy, grey gun smoke.

It was on what would be those ill-defined ridges that the Allied troops had been deployed, and both Wilson and Papagos were peering through their binoculars to see that they were all situated correctly.

"Good!" Wilson said when he saw that Australia's 2/8 Battalion, as part of Vasey's 19th Brigade, was now positioned to guard the vital Pass leading to Vevi.

While Papagos, with his magnified view of the topography, could confirm that his 4.500 strong Greek Dodecanese Regiment had set up successfully near Lakes Vegorritis and Petron, so that it could link up with the 2/8 as fast as possible.

The British 1st Rangers were stationed on the main road, while with the backing of the 21st Greek Brigade, a strong contingent of Anzac and British artillery were standing steady at the centre.

"Pity the same can't be said for the Australian 2/4," Wilson added, having to huff on his binocular lenses and swipe them clean with his sleeve to get a clearer view of Vasey's other battalion that, due to its shortage of troops, was spread so thin over the six-kilometre front on the hills to the left.

The main battle, as yet, wasn't underway, but in preparation for what was to come, the destruction had already begun. Australian field engineers had blown up the railway and bridge servicing the valley, and to further protect the Allied troops, were now busy blasting big holes in the main road and laying a minefield in advance of their defensive position.

Meanwhile, despite being positioned on their hill as planned, the 2/8 Battalion was still at a distinct disadvantage. Not only numerically, but because they'd been forced to march for miles through mud and mountainous terrain, and having done it without rest to get to the battle in time, were on the brink of exhaustion. In their bid to protect Greece's northern border, they'd had to move at double-pace, with those who collapsed along the way, relying on their fellow soldiers to quickly redistribute their gear and lend a supportive shoulder.

It would have been worth the effort had their destination not given them such a cold reception. For the mountain was caked in snow, metres-thick, presenting them with a prospective battlefield of icy, wet white – a sight and situation that most of them from warmer climes had neither seen nor experienced before. Yet, with the SS due to hit them hard the next morning, they were expected to fight knee-deep in it, suffering from frostbite and the frustration of firearms jammed-frozen and refusing to fire.

CHAPTER 21

THE ATTACK ON THEIR HILL 997 came at dawn, and after hours of fierce fighting, an entire company was forced to withdraw, because its 14th platoon had been decimated with only six of its men left alive.

Those men from that annihilated platoon had been having their first breakfast in days when they were interrupted by German shelling and the SS infantry following hard behind. They were caught on the hop and in big trouble, but when, in the emergency of the moment, their young commanding officer, Lieutenant Tommy Oldfield, heroically pulled his service revolver and moved to lead them out into the open, his men were horrified.

"For Christ's sake Tommy, come back!" the more experienced Sergeant Bob Slocombe yelled out after him.

But Oldfield didn't hear, because within seconds he was dead.

The rest of the platoon was next on the German's hit list, and with many of its sections already overrun, Slocombe and a few others fought their way to the safety of a reverse slope, where they, in their pitiful numbers, held off the huge enemy force until noon.

It was a show of superhuman strength on their part, given that they saw it as their last stand, and with nothing left to lose, they just got angry and gave it all they'd got.

"It's likely none of us will survive," Slocombe said to his small band of men at the start. "But if we're gonna go down, we're gonna take as many of them with us as we can."

They were fully expecting to die, which made them all the more amazed when the Germans suddenly moved off and let them live another day. Although breathing a sigh of relief, their death-defying bad moods wouldn't have been appeased had they known that, back at 6 Division's headquarters, their life-and-death struggle was being written off as *'a slight penetration of defenses'*.

By noon, the Germans were spilling over nearby Hill 917, where despite putting up a good show, another company from the 2/8 finally succumbed to the enemy's superior forces and fell back.

Nothing, for the Allies, was going well, but they would have been faring better had the battles going on all over the war zone not been hampered by miscommunication that was making a complete mess of things.

"Australia's 2/8 is retreating," the commander of the British 1st Rangers was told.

In response to this piece of poor information, he replied:

"Well, in that case, we'd better do the same."

It was a fatal decision that opened the vital Klidi Pass to the Germans, not only creating a gap between Australia's 2/4 and 2/8 Battalions, but severing communications with their commander, Vasey, while leaving Australian anti-tank guns without infantry protection.

When Vasey was finally informed by other units that the Rangers had withdrawn, he couldn't believe it.

"What bloody fool told them to do that!" he bellowed, in what was always his ripe language in an emergency.

It was a move, however, for which the Rangers couldn't be blamed when most communications were down and no one could work out what was going on.

"We've lost contact with the Australian 2/4, and all Allied troops are falling back," the Greek 21st Infantry reported over their fast-fading radio, while those trying to listen to their thick accents through the static were wondering whether they heard it right.

It would have been bad news had it been true, but the reality was that while two of the 2/8's companies had been forced to retreat, what was left of the battalion had made a counter-attack and regained vital ground. After much intermittent fighting, they still held the Hills, even though their left flank had been mauled.

It was, however, a last hurrah, for the Allies were on the back foot, with the British Rangers, although having rallied two miles to the rear, finding themselves without support. It was the final blow for them to find out that the six big guns from the 2/1 Anti-Tank Regiment on which they'd been relying had been abandoned and were sitting idle in the middle of the main road.

"It's time to go," both the British and Greeks decided, but their sudden departure left Australia's 2/8 Battalion exposed on both flanks. By mid afternoon, its men were coming under intense machine-gun fire, with all of them worn out and with no hope of being relieved.

Any chance of winning the battle was long gone, and seeing that his men were beyond even staging an orderly withdrawal, Vasey put through a call to his 2/4 Battalion, and speaking to its commanding officer, Lieutenant Colonel Percival Parsons, used the code indicating that a pull-out was now imperative:

"Percy," he said."The roof is leaking."

CHAPTER 22

"FALL BACK FAST!"

That final order put an end to the 2/8 Battalion as a fighting force for the rest of the Greek campaign, for during its haphazard retreat many of its men went missing, along with their munitions. By the time the remnants of the battalion reached their pullout position, only 250 of its full complement of 900 could be mustered. Just fifty of them were still carrying rifles.

The rest, as they fled, lost sight of them before getting to Tempe Gorge, where Australia's 16th Brigade was setting up to make a stand under the command of Brigadier "Tubby" Allen. A man who'd been so brilliant and brave in WWI, and for whom his men had such affection, that it seemed a shame that neither he nor they knew what horrors lay ahead of them. That before long they'd hear the rumble of 1000 German tanks, and that soon after, 200 of their own troops would become casualties of war for trying to stand in their way. Those retreating from Vevi were without the weapons or energy to help, so the best they could do was warn them.

"Get the hell out boys ... they're not taking prisoners!" a survivor from the 2/8 said as he limped by.

But fresh-faced and full of bravado, one of the 16th's soldiers shouted back:

"Bugger you. We're staying."

Further north, other soldiers from 6 Division were doing better falling back from Servia Pass, contrary to the hell of a time they'd had getting there.

–oOo–

"Send your brigade's transports back to the village of Gerania," Blamey had ordered at the time.

He had good reasons for issuing this command, but it meant that three Australian battalions had to make their way, on foot, up and over a 1000-metre mountain range slathered in snow and sludge.

"It'll toughen them up and be better than the German ambush they'd get taking the alternative route," Blamey said in explanation to Brigadier Sydney Rowell, who as his chief of staff, wasn't at all sure he was right.

It wasn't the first time Rowell had silently questioned Blamey's initiatives, but he wasn't brave enough, as yet, to speak out against them. His better instincts, however, were smack on track, unlike one of those three walking battalions which, during a blizzard, completely lost sight of their path and fellow battalions. For what seemed like a long, desperate time, they were left wandering in the white wilderness, where the unbearable cold and high altitude forced them to leave most of their equipment and ammunition behind.

Fortunately, the two other battalions had found the right

road to follow, but they were fast running out of rations and had to resort to stealing the Greek food offerings at shrines along the way. In doing so, they risked God's wrath, but somehow they didn't care when they were sure they were already in hell, marching without overcoats and with just one ground-sheet each on which to sleep in the four-foot deep snow.

"We march in it, sleep in it, and suffer in it," one soldier said feeling defeated.

In answer to which, his platoon sergeant offered some sage advice:

"Always change your socks whenever you can."

Under their dire circumstances, it seemed a feeble piece of advice, but oddly enough it helped, despite the soldiers' socks being as snap-frozen as their feet.

Surely, they thought, *things couldn't go downhill from here.*

But then the rains came, and hardening overnight, left sheets of ice over them in place of blankets.

It was a wonder any of them survived, and when one of them collapsed and looked as if he wouldn't, Private Bill Jenkins doubled back in a brave effort to save him.

Having to trudge through the snow with the burden of another man on his back, meant that it took him and his sick companion two days to catch up with their rearguard artillery. By then, Jenkins was so numb with cold and exhaustion that he jumped on the hot barrel of a 60-pound gun and hugged it to thaw out.

Every shivering solder watching on couldn't blame him, but when he told them that, for the sake of the man he'd saved, he'd left the troops' tea and sugar rations behind, they weren't happy and didn't give a bugger about his heroics:

"You stupid bastard!" one of them said, before he and rest refused to speak to him.[23]

CHAPTER 23

THEY HAD MANAGED, however, to reach their position near Servia, and although the weather was still brutal, their vantage point on the heights was excellent, while the ground around Mt Olympus worked to their advantage. Luck later went with them in their retreat thanks to the mountain passes offering safety and natural defensive positions from which they further delayed the enemy. They knew, though, that they were playing a losing game, and while in retreat, were relying on all Anzac troops to rally round in whichever way they could.

"Look out for the Luftwaffe," Captain Ian Manson of Australia's 2/1 battalion was warned by a Kiwi officer only seconds before a Messerschmitt came screaming over the ridge spitting fire from its wings.[24]

Manson hit the ground, and flinging his arms over his head for protection was saved from the rapid spray of bullets, but those standing near him, who didn't have the sense to do the same, didn't fare so well. Nonetheless, one Anzac had saved another, and to repay the favour, a small band of Australians obliged by blowing up the bridge over the Aliakmon River to stop the Nazi's 9th Panzer rolling its way over it and ruining the Kiwis' retreat.

In the meantime, casualties from the Battle of Vevi were rolling in, and doing so in such vast numbers that the field hospital couldn't cope: During her brief break from the flood of blood and men, Nurse Mollie Edwards wrote a note to a friend:

> *All I can do is hold each man's hand as he dies. Every peacetime procedure has gone out the window, with us unable to wait for doctors, but having to diagnose and administer the drugs ourselves. Last night, the doctor simply handed me the morphine and syringe and said 'get on with it!'* [25]

Their Anzac retreat was in disarray, and while they backed away, fighting for the lives, Blamey was at his headquarters in the Greek town of Elasson, where he'd just received the latest battle update. He'd been keeping close tabs on the trials of Mackay's 6th Division, but as he read what had happened to Vasey's two besieged battalions, he could barely contain his dismay:

> *Although Mackay's troops have been defeated and his 6th Division has suffered heavy losses, its actions at Vevi have gained two days for the retreat and regrouping of Allied forces to the south.*

It took a short moment for the news of their defeat to sink in, but then Blamey made the most of it.

"Well, at least we've achieved our objectives and there's something to be said for that."

The fact that Vasey's 2/4 Battalion had been outflanked and forced to withdraw due to the collapse of all surrounding support was the least of it. The worst was that, in just two days, the Battle of Vevi had notched up close to 600 Allied casualties – dead, wounded or gone missing. At this point, Blamey could only assume that most of them were his Australians.

He was usually a cold, hard man, but right now, the sentimentality that was sometimes stirred by those under his command had him fight back hot tears of rage. For they were his men and his responsibility, yet ever since they'd arrived in Greece and seen the sorry state of its Port Piraeus, he'd known that nothing for them could possibly go well.

–oOo–

"Looks like we'll be on a hiding to nothing here," one soldier had said to another when their Australian troopship sailed into the near-annihilated Greek harbour.

It was clear that the Luftwaffe had been there before them, because the coves that had served the country so well since ancient times had been flattened. What the Persian and Peloponnesian Wars of the past had failed to destroy had now been reduced to rubble by only a handful of German bombers, with just one pilot from the small squadron laying claim to the cataclysmic destruction of the port being used for the main build-up of British forces.

"Leave that big boy to me," Hauptmann Hajo Herrmann had transmitted to his Staffel 7, before putting his Junkers Ju 88 bomber into a steep dive to attack at close quarters.

"Bullseye!" he then boasted to his fellow flyers, when the three bombs he dropped landed front and centre of the huge freighter docked by the quay.

He didn't know that he'd struck it lucky – that the ship was only half unloaded and what remained on its now burning decks was 250 tons of TNT destined for the Greek ammunition plants.

The impact of his bombs literally lifted the ship out of the water and snapped her mooring lines in half. She was adrift and ablaze, and with her steel sides glowing fluorescent with internal heat, men burned black by the flames were falling dead on her decks, while those still alive leapt like human torches into the sea. It was a scene of such stark horror, that it was a mercy when she exploded.

The gargantuan blast ricocheted around the bay killing hundreds of sailors, soldiers and civilians, while setting in motion the sympathetic sinking of 12 other ships. Every inch of Piraeus was leveled, and as glass windows shattered in Athens, 11 kilometres away, a red, demonic glow lit up its Acropolis.

Overhead, Herrmann's plane was being hurled about in the sky with the aftershock of the blast having damaged its engine. Not badly enough, however, to stop him limping, triumphantly back to base with his Staffel and swastikas.[26]

It took ten days for the Port of Piraeus to be back in operation, but its burning embers and rancid smell of death hadn't augured well when, soon after, Australian troops arrived.

CHAPTER 24

THERE WASN'T MUCH BENEFIT for Blamey in leading the losing side, but he had to remember that the greatest man in military history made his name doing the same. That King Leonidas with his 300 Spartans, just like he and his Australians, were tasked to guard the Thermopylae Pass as a last line of defence against impossible odds.

For the ancient Greeks, it was a case of do and die, but fortunately, for Blamey and his men, there was a 'get-out clause' in that those who survived could retreat. It was just as well, for while the Spartan story of supreme sacrifice had since lit a fire in every schoolboy's heart, the prospect of a modern-day re-run wasn't so appealing to the fighting-too-far-from-home Australians.

They had been ordered to hold the enemy at the Pass until the rest of the Allies got away. But to remove those Allies from Greece was a logistical nightmare, with the Germans hot on their heels and the Luftwaffe taking unfair advantage of shooting down those retreating on foot from the safety of their cockpits. Had communications been good, it would have helped, but with most of them down, the troops scattered all over the country were without direction from the military, or in regard to their location.

Blamey was in control of the withdrawal, and theoretically, it couldn't have been in better hands, because when it came to organisational skills, his were second to none and there was no one more suitable to sort out the situation.

Blamey's index finger, right now, was pointing to the city of Larissa on their military map.

"Here's the choking point," he said to the Commander of New Zealand's army, Major General Bernard Freyberg. "All roads meet at this junction, and with the bulk of our troops converging on it, there could be chaos. Somehow, we have to stop any congestion, and at the same time, block the Germans from using the road for their advance."

They both agreed it was vital ground, and with the 9th Panzer Division moving rapidly towards them, Blamey sent his reliable old friend, Brigadier Stanley Savige with his 17th Brigade, to monitor the situation while Greece fell to pieces around them.

The whole country was on the point of collapse, with its own soldiers on their last legs for having fought fiercely without respite, and its starving citizens being shot for supporting them with everything they had. For the sake of what was left of his nation's proud people and heritage, Greek Commander-in-Chief Papagos made the only sensible decision:

"I want all Allied troops to leave," he said, knowing that if they didn't, Greece and all for which it stood over the centuries would be obliterated.

At his headquarters in Cairo, Commander-in-Chief of the Middle East, General Wavell agreed, because Greece, he'd always known, was a lost cause and a waste of soldiers and resources that could be better used elsewhere. Namely, in his own Western

Desert Campaign, which they, the Allies, had at least half a chance of winning.

To that end, all support and supply to Greece ceased, and feeling less burdened by its constant bad news, Wavell sent a last note to General Wilson, ordering him to wrap up what had been the whole disastrous Greek Campaign:

> *Finish up at Thermopylae as fast as possible and move your troops to Crete. They are to hold that island until further notice.*

Much as they wanted to go, it was hard for the Australians to say goodbye for they felt they were forsaking the Greeks with whom they had bonded.

"We're so sorry, but we're under orders to leave," one soldier stopped to say to an old woman, as he and his Anzac battalion marched in retreat through her village.

God only knew what lay ahead of her and the rest of its inhabitants with the Germans only a few miles behind, Yet, despite the fear and hunger in her hollowed eyes, there wasn't within them a hint of condemnation. Instead, she handed him her last loaf of bread and said:

"Thank you for trying to save us."

If they had, it had only been for a short time, for during the German invasion and occupation, 540,000 Greeks were to perish from war wounds, reprisal killings and starvation, while those among them who were Jews were to suffer far more and die dreadful deaths in German concentration camps.

CHAPTER 25

AS THEIR LAST OFFERING of help, the Anzacs still had one stop to make before they left. Wavell's directive in regard to it seemed clear enough, but the reality of 'finishing up at Thermopylae' wasn't that simple.

The last thing Britain wanted was another Dunkirk, so to make sure this evacuation didn't go the same way, they told the Anzacs to keep the Germans at bay while it happened. It was a tall order, but at least those Anzacs knew that Thermopylae was a defenders' dream – a 1200-metre escarpment, which rising from the central Greek plain, formed a natural barrier. While Thermopylae itself was to be guarded by a New Zealand division, Vasey's Australian 19th Brigade was to protect the pivotal Brallos Pass. It was the crucial rearguard position of the whole Thermopylae defence, and having regained their breath after the Battle of Vevi, Vasey's men were out for revenge and set on taking a second, more successful shot at the enemy.

That enemy, by now, had caught up with them, and while one of its German divisions had Vasey's 2/11 battalion pinned down under intense fire, another was moving along the railway line to attack Brallos from the West. There, Australia's 2/1 Machine Gun Battalion was stationed in support, with its men and Vickers guns standing at the ready. They fought well for some time through the ensuing firefight, but the Germans soon grew sick of the stalemate, and rolling in their heavy mortars, brought the 2/1 Battalion's left flank to its knees.

"*Why us?*" one of its lieutenants shouted at Vasey when, in the heat of battle, three of his men were blown apart.

To this, in his usual hard-line way, Vasey swore in reply:

"Because here we bloody well are, and here we bloody well stay! And if any bloody German gets between your post and the next, turn your bloody bren around and shoot him up the arse!"

A few more of his expletives followed, and if their situation hadn't been so dire, his men would have laughed.

"There's no one like Vasey to buck us up when we're down," one soldier said, because they'd come to rely and his colourful command, and knew that, without it, they'd be lost.

In this instance, his coarse words humoured them into holding out long enough for their supporting artillery to escape intact. While bit by bit, by way of their fight-and-flight, leap-frog tactics, the 19th Brigade, as a whole, was being slowly withdrawn right under the enemy's nose.

"But we'd better pace it up," Vasey said to his second-in-command. 'It won't be long before they break through our defences."

The systematic departure of his 2/11, however, left the guns of the 2/2 Field Regiment exposed. An unfortunate consequence that forced the Commander of the Australian Artillery, Lieutenant Colonel William Cremor, to take drastic measures:

"Fire on the 2/11's vacated ground," he ordered during the short silence between attacks.

It was a command so extraordinary that Major Jaboor of the 3rd Battery hesitated.

"Sir," he said. "We don't even know whether all its men have pulled out."

At his orders being questioned, Cremor turned on him with a cold, deathly calm and replied:

"Do what you're told and bring down fire."

His tone left no room for dispute, so as the gunners began their barrage, they could only pray that their fellow soldiers had got out in time. Hard as it was to carry out the command, it was the right one, for not only had the men of 2/11 escaped unscathed, but the bombardment went further to save their skins by stopping the Germans coming after them across the fire-swept ground they'd left behind.[27]

For a short time, then, the Australians took the offensive, turning their 25-pounders to fire down the railway tunnel through which the enemy was now advancing.

"Just like shooting fish in a barrel," one gunner said, because it made for such easy pickings, aiming his gun at the big, black hole at the tunnel's entrance and shooting down every Kraut who came out.

The bodies of those dead Germans dammed up the railway tracks and slowed the rest of their divisions down. Yet, rather than feeling bitter, their German commanders were full of praise for their enemy's performance. So much so, that one of them wrote about it in his report:

> *We are so impressed by the Australians' expertise: By their shooting precision and the backing of their skilled defence as their units make rearward leaps. Due to that smart strategy, we now face miles of their road demolitions if we are to have any hope of catching up with their rearguard.*[28]

It had been hard-earned praise that was to stand the test of time, for sixty years after the war, those Australians would still say:

"We were proud of what we did that day."

CHAPTER 26

MEANWHILE, MAJOR GENERAL FREYBERG'S New Zealand Division was doing a first-rate job fighting the Battle of Thermopylae 20th century style.

The Germans, as part of their' plan to encircle the Australians, had sent tanks and infantry to assault the position, but they didn't reckon on running up against the resolute Kiwi troops guarding it or the difficult terrain that forced their Panzers to go through the Pass in single file.

"And bang, bang, you're dead!" one Kiwi corporal said, as he took aim and fired on the tanks rolling past their 25-pounders. Like a shooting gallery of sitting ducks, he was knocking them out, one after the other in quick succession, while the German infantry following in their wake fared no better.

What had been a dead-man's game for the Anzacs had been changed to success, with their defence of Thermopylae and Brallos barring the enemy's way while the rest of the Allies got safely south. The Germans were so incensed that, in one monumental temper tantrum, they sent 50 of their Luftwaffe planes to plaster both positions, so that any Anzacs still there would get exactly what they deserved.

Fortunately, by then, all Anzacs were gone, and with every one of them racing to reach the evacuation beaches in time, they had none of it left to dwell on what had been their outstanding performance. Many of them wouldn't make it, while those who did had to spend what was their sacred Anzac Day of April 25, dodging Messerschmitts and sheltering in olive groves behind the beaches until embarkation.

Some six hundred less lucky missed the last rescue ship and had to find their own way home, which meant crossing a continent crawling with Nazis without food or money, or the correct language and civilian clothes to cover their identities. However, they believed anything was better than suffering the fate of their fellow soldiers. Seventeen hundred of whom were dead or wounded, while the 5000 left behind were to be taken prisoners of war.

It was some rotten reward for their three weeks of battle without respite, while constantly having to move position. With each of those moves being in retreat, there'd been no time to reconnoitre or prepare their defensive posts. Yet somehow, through what was the most critical point of the campaign, they'd managed to fight the more experienced and better equipped Germans to a standstill.

Blamey was proud of that when he read the latest army update. Yet, wonderful as it was to know, there was still better news for him to come, and it came by way of General Wilson's written order from Athens:

> *You are not to assume the obligation of the Anzac Corps evacuation, but are to report immediately, instead, to headquarters in Cairo.*

It was Wilson's most incomprehensible command of the campaign, and that was saying something, when during its course his ineptitude had seen him issue so many almost as inane. For a short moment, Blamey stood stunned by its implication.

"In other words," he then said out loud. "I am to desert my troops and fly myself to safety."

The dismissive guffaw he let out in response said there was fat chance of that, but then he read on and saw what was in it for him:

> *All senior commanders are to accompany you, for it would not do for them to be there at the Allied departure from Greece. They should also be in Egypt, to witness your promotion to the rank of Deputy Commander-in-Chief of Middle East Command.*

With that astounding piece of information, Wilson signed off, but then added an important P.S.:

> *Pease limit the members of your personal staff to three due to shortage of seats on the plane.*

Blamey knew that the British War Office had trumped up his new title to stop him throwing a spanner in the works. They were sick of him being so bloody-minded about what was best for his Australian troops, forever insisting that they fight as one and not be broken up and spread thin, when it served Britain's purpose to do just that. They'd finally found out that the only way to budge Blamey on military matters was via his ego.

CHAPTER 27

"BUT YOU CAN'T JUST LEAVE like that!" his Chief of Staff Rowell said, stopping short of calling Blamey a coward.

"I have no option," he answered. "I'm under orders to go, as are you."

At this, Rowell stepped back in outrage, and for the first time in his exemplary military career, dared to disobey orders:

"Well that, sir, I flatly refuse to do. Court martial me if you like, but I will not run out on our men and shall stay to do all I can to see to their safe evacuation."

"Aren't you forgetting who's in command here?" Blamey flashed back in fury. "And that it's your duty to follow my orders?"

It was hardly something Blamey could fling in Rowell's face when he had just forsaken that command, but he was shocked that Rowell had spoken out against him when he'd always been his right-hand man and given his unstinting support.

This sudden defiance on Rowell's part had now effectively set up what would be a lifelong rift between them. One over which neither would back down, while being bad enough for

Rowell to lose all respect for Blamey as a commander, and basically, as a man.

Major General Mackay, as Commander of the 6th Division, was subject to the same fast-exit order, as was New Zealand's Lieutenant-General Freyberg, but while Mackay followed the directive, Freyberg, like Rowell, refused to go.

"I will not desert my men to save myself," he said, and Blamey didn't even bother to argue, because he knew Freyberg was as stubborn as he and meant business.

Both Rowell's and Freyberg's words were said to shame him, and perhaps they would have if Blamey didn't have his eye on the big picture. It was one he would have happily shared with them, had he not been sure that building his own career from the wreckage of their Greek campaign wouldn't go down well with them.[29]

Neither man, however, would ever publicly bad-mouth him, and when Freyberg was later asked his opinion on the subject, he let others draw their own conclusion by keeping his words to a minimum:

"Blamey left. I didn't."

For the rest of his life, Blamey would have a lot to be embarrassed about, for if fleeing the scene wasn't ignoble enough, he then added insult to injury in his treatment of his troops on his way out.

–oOo–

"The old bastard's taking his son with him!" one soldier called out with contempt as Blamey and his entourage walked past their exhausted ranks on their way to boarding the seaplane.

That son of his, young Major Tom Blamey, had no choice in the matter, and under the awkward circumstances, found it hard to follow behind his father with his eyes cast down and ears blocked to what he, too, believed was fair condemnation.

He had to keep those eyes of his averted as they moved past a stretcher-bound soldier lying with his bandages soaked in blood. A Lieutenant Gwynne Mann, who'd been wounded once at the Battle of Bardia, and now a second time in Greece for having heroically saved the lives of his whole platoon.[30]

"This man's lost his leg winning the military cross." one of his stretcher-bearers said to Blamey as he strode by. "Can't you find just a small space for him on your plane?"

Blamey stopped, and with respect saluted the soldier before walking on.

"He's scared out of his life," Rowell said to Vasey as they watched him go.

"Yes, but to include his boy is just too terrible," Vasey replied. "He has disgraced both himself and his son by doing so."[31]

CHAPTER 28

BAD NEWS TRAVELLED FAST on the military network, and when Lavarack heard what had happened, he couldn't help but feel sorry for Blamey. While every Australian soldier and civilian was scandlised by his behaviour, he knew that Blamey, having already lost one son to the war, had risked all to save his other.

With three sons of his own, Lavarack was sure he would have done the same, but considering the ongoing enmity between them, he surprised even himself by how fast he leapt to Blamey's defence.

"There's not a cowardly bone in that man's body," his said in angry response to the damning reports.

However, he should have spared himself his finer feelings, for not only was Blamey destined to, yet again, fall on his feet, but in having secured his impressive promotion, he didn't care about the criticism, or even the fact that he had to hand over his old command to the man he disliked the most.

Lavarack, with his 7th Division, had been in Syria since leaving Tobruk, and while the disastrous Battles of Greece and Crete were being fought and lost without him, he'd been busy with battles of his own. He was midway through one of them when he was told to take over Blamey's prior role as Commander of Australia's I Corps.

It was good news that Lavarack couldn't take completely on board until he finished combating General Wilson over an order he'd issued that wouldn't work.

"Your attack plan for Syria and Lebanon is faulty," he'd warned Wilson repeatedly, but with the man still not listening, he said it again:

"The routes you've designated for my 7th Division to advance are just inviting disaster."

Wilson, however, still wasn't convinced that the enemy they were facing would put up much of a defence, so Lavarack had to help him along with his power of comprehension by continuing as diplomatically as he could.

"We should, I think sir, have a more realistic appreciation of how the Vichy French will react to such an advance."

With his words falling again on deaf ear, Lavarack took matters into his own hands, and for the sake of his troops, allotted his 2/25 Divisional Reserve Battalion to his 25th Brigade as back up.

The move made all the difference as he and his 7th advanced up Lebanon's coast and inland roads. While in a second master stroke, Lavarack seized the opportunity to suddenly change the axis of their advance by thrusting towards the town of Jezzine where they caught the enemy unawares.

It had been during the French counterattack that Lavarack took on his promotion, again, to the rank of Lieutenant General, along with the command of Australia's 1 Corps. With that command came the responsibility for almost the entire Syrian Campaign, and now with the 7th Division, as well as the British,

Indian and Free French under his wing, he would oversee the capture of Damascus and Damour, and within 26 days, an armistice.

"The man has displayed abilities of the highest order," Wavell said of Lavarack at his Cairo headquarters, while soon after making sure that this outstanding Australian commander was appointed K.B.E and mentioned in dispatches.

"Which, if I had my way," Wavell went on to say, "would be done in bold print."

PART FOUR

TALES OF THE SOUTH WEST PACIFIC

CHAPTER 29

IT WAS A MID-WINTER MONDAY when, with solemn resolve, President Franklin D. Roosevelt addressed his nation:

"Yesterday, December 7th, 1941, a date which will live in infamy, the United States of America was suddenly and deliberately attacked by naval and air forces of the Empire of Japan."

The news of the unprecedented attacks on Pearl Harbour and Malaya meant that America, at long last, was committed to the war and that the Australians, who'd been fighting it for some time, had to say farewell to fellow Allied troops in Europe and beat a hasty retreat back home.

"Well that's it for us boys!" they said as they swiftly gathered up their gear. "We've done our bit here, but now we have to move like lighting to protect our own."

Australia, always so safe in its seclusion, was suddenly under threat of invasion, and as a matter of emergency, both its 6th and 7th Divisions had been recalled from the Middle East, while its 9th, still fighting in North Africa, was on standby to follow suit.

Though many Australian troops, including its RAAF, were to remain in the European theatre or war,[32] it was little wonder that the British War Office was dismayed by this abrupt removal of such a mighty fighting force from the front, but their strong objection to it didn't go down well.

"We believe that your soldiers are duty-bound to stay," their Secretary of State for War said to instill a sense of guilt that might stall the process.[33]

His having even suggested as much in such a crisis, however, sparked a heated political debate with Australia's new Prime Minister, John Curtin; a man, who as the polar opposite of his predecessor, Robert Menzies, was all for Australia, rather than wanting to appease England.

"I insist on the immediate return of our infantry divisions," he fired back in red hot response, "Their battle-hardened troops are crucial to Australia's defence."

It was at this point that Prime Minister Winston Churchill weighed in on the argument.

"It would be far more beneficial for all concerned if your 7th Division were deployed to Burma."

Curtin, however, couldn't be swayed, for in both world wars Australian troops had given their all for other countries and he considered it an outrage that those same countries should now stop them defending their own.

Britain had made a big mistake in wiping aside its prior colony's plight, for after 170 years of giving the Mother Country its full support, Australia now got sensible and switched its foreign policy focus to America.

"It was bound to happen someday," Churchill confided to his close associates. "Their countries are nearer in proximity, and with both bordering and having a vested interest in the Pacific, an alliance between them was inevitable."

Beyond being a realist, however, Churchill was a man who never let go of a bone, and somehow managed to negotiate a short-term compromise.

"Would you consider," he asked Curtin in a more conciliatory tone, "deploying just part of your 6th Division to Ceylon, so that Japanese expansion can be checked, at least within that region?"

In consideration of that more appropriate tone and the bonds that had long been between them, Curtin agreed. It was a concession, though, that wasn't to last, for by July, both brigades diverted there,[34] would be urgently needed to help hold back the hordes of Japanese troops pouring into New Guinea as their gateway to Australia.

Lavarack, meanwhile, had to admit that he agreed with Churchill about Burma.

"I think that putting our efforts into holding Burma is the best way to go," he said during a meeting at General Wavell's new headquarters in West Java.

All present were happy to hear him say it and urged him to continue.

"If we can leave the Burma Road open," he followed on, "it will keep China in the war, and that's imperative, because with most of Japan's Imperial Army deployed and bogged down there, their advance into the Asia-Pacific region will pretty much grind to a halt."

In this instance, Lavarack was on Britain's side, but that's where his support for its overall strategy stopped.

"I don't, however, believe that we should send more troops to the Dutch East Indies, because it will prove hopeless."

Wavell now sat bolt upright in his seat to object:

"I say, that with the Japanese advancing so fast down Malaya, the best we can hope for is to hold Singapore. The way to do it is to send one of your Australian divisions to Sumatra, while making sure that another stays here in Java."

As to that, Lavarack strongly protested.

"It'd be much better if my 1 Corps stayed together," he argued. "The Dutch East Indies Army is totally unreliable. Its men are badly trained, poorly armed, and of questionable loyalty, with most of its Indonesian troops close to rebelling against their Dutch officers."

Though the situation was of concern, Wavell felt confident in his reply:

"Well, considering the Japanese threat to their own nation, I'm sure they'll be brought into line."

It seemed a logical expectation, so Wavell was surprised when Lavarack wiped his words aside with a dismissive sweep of his hand, and then took a few steps closer to look him directly in the eye.

"Of this, sir, you can be certain," he stated. "The Indonesian troops will not fight against their fellow Asians. Even as we speak, they are embracing Japan's slogan of *Asia for Asians!* If we are to adopt your plan, there's no doubt that Australians will have to bear the brunt of the fighting."

That prospect didn't worry Wavell too much. What did, was the fact that he'd recently cast Lavarack in a golden light, while now the man was all storm and thunder and not showing him due respect.

CHAPTER 30

"DOES THAT MAN of yours, Lavarack, always express his opinion so decidedly?" Wavell later asked Blamey.

"Ceaselessly!" he answered, with the inference of rolling his eyes.

"Well, you must stop him doing it, because it's interfering with my plans for Java."

To stop Lavarack speaking his mind was something Blamey had never been able to do, but it didn't really matter when Wavell had already made up his mind:

"Contrary to Lieutenant General Lavarack's advice," he said, "I have ordered two battalions from his 7th Division[35] to guard the airstrip at Java's capital of Batavia."

It was a bad move on Wavell's part, and like Lavarack, Blamey baulked at the likelihood that it would cost Australia both those battalions.

"Who's in command of them?" he whispered hastily to his ADC, Captain Norman Carlyon.

"Blackburn, sir," Carlyon answered.

Instantly, Blamey's mind was set at rest.

"Good," he said. "He's the one man who might have a chance of seeing them through."

–oOo–

Blamey had never forgotten Blackburn, or the fact that he'd won the Victoria Cross for conspicuous gallantry at The Great War's Battle of Pozieres. Blackburn had been a second lieutenant back then, but now, as a brigadier, was about to show the same outstanding courage by saving his men from what was, in every practical sense, a suicide mission.

He and his unit were on their way back to Australia when their troopship was suddenly diverted to Java. There was a sense of emergency in the air, and as soon as Blackburn set foot on shore, he was put in command of "Blackforce', named in his honour, and given the responsibility of a 3,000-strong force.

"You are to protect Batavia's airstrip," he was told by Wavell, who seemed strangely on edge.

The reason soon became clear, for although the mission would normally have been easy to carry out, it had now been made impossible, because the Japanese had just taken Singapore and were bombing the heck out of Australia's city of Darwin.

"Which means that our troops will have to move even faster to get home," Australia's Prime Minister decreed, with the situation now too close for comfort.

Unfortunately, for the sake of Australia, it meant leaving Blackburn and his men to their fate in Java. By March, 1942, they'd been overwhelmed by the sheer immensity of enemy numbers and all 3000 of them, forced to surrender, were taken prisoners.

To be subjected to as much, under Japanese rule, was the same as a death sentence, but Blackburn wasn't about to let it end there and was probably the first and only man in history to earn a knighthood for talking the enemy round. Without the benefit of weapons, or giving a toss about his own safety, he was to turn defeat to a win by constantly standing up to his Japanese jailers. Despite them trying to starve and beat him into submission, he kept getting to his feet and voicing his opinion so strongly in regard to their maltreatment that he eventually managed to bully the Japanese into behaving.

CHAPTER 31

THE ENEMY'S RAPID ADVANCE, along with this strange new thing called: 'war on our own doorstep', had Australians alarmed, so it helped to know that their troops were coming to save them. For Rowell, however, who'd been recalled some time before them, returning home wasn't so sweet. He should have been proud of being promoted to the rank of major general and his new role as Deputy Chief of the General Staff, but after all his valiant efforts to stay with his troops in Greece, he was disappointed.

'Poor Syd," Vasey said, feeling sorry for his old friend. "He was pulled out of The Great War way too early and now it looks like he won't see much of the Second."[36]

His words couldn't have been more wrong, for within four months, Rowell and so many other Australians would be in the thick of it. Meanwhile, Rowell and his superior, Chief of the General Staff, Lieutenant General Vernon Sturdee, were going flat out to fast-track Australia's defences before Japan broke down its door. They were working at such a frenetic pace, that it wasn't the time for Vasey and other senior officers to put forward a radical new plan:

"This campaign is going to be more demanding than any we've fought before," Vasey said, in his usual forthright way. "For that reason, we recommend the retirement of all generals over the age of 50 in favour of younger, energetic men more physically and mentally equipped to take on the trying, tropical conditions."

Here, Vasey paused to permit a response, but with Rowell stunned silent, he then continued:

"In accordance, we believe that Major General Horace Robertson should be made Commander-in-Chief."

It was a convenient recommendation given that 48-year-old Robertson and Vasey, at 46, were still young enough to scrape through selection. Yet, beyond being expedient, it seemed a sensible solution to what lay ahead, so Vasey was surprised that Rowell, as his trusted friend and fellow Duntroon graduate, wasn't in support and saw their bold initiative as going a step too far.

"This ill-timed, little Generals' Revolt of yours couldn't be more lousy," Rowell suddenly said, having found his voice in fury. "If you weren't so bloody big Vasey, I'd hurl you out of my office."

It was at this point in their heated debate that Generals Sturdee and Lavarack walked into the room.

"What's going on?" their raised eyebrows asked on seeing angry faces all round.

After an awkward silence, Rowell gestured toward Vasey, giving him the floor to voice his controversial proposal.

Lavarack may well have thought it was a good one had he not been 57, or if he, himself, hadn't just been appointed Acting Commander-in-Chief until Blamey returned from the Middle East.

One thing was for sure – when Blamey came back to claim the title, he would be decidedly against it, for despite being well over 50 and sporting a body now much wider around the girth, he was still fighting fit and ready to take on the world.

"I don't know how he does it," younger, seemingly stronger men kept saying, because by pure grit determination and endurance, Blamey could outdo them all and took great pride in issuing the challenge to anyone who even hinted at him not being up to the task.

CHAPTER 32

BLAMEY WAS WONDERING, all the way home, whether he'd be welcome back in Australia after having fled Greece, but there was no need to worry when, as always, he was to bounce back from his bad situation.

The second he arrived, all rumours of cowardice and malicious gossip against him were miraculously forgotten, while those who'd been quick to condemn him before Japan declared war, now said they missed him and couldn't wait till he was crowned Commander-in-Chief of the Australian Military Forces and of the Allied Land Forces in the South West Pacific. As such, in military matters, he was answerable to just one man – the American in overall command, General Douglas MacArthur.

Singapore had fallen to Japan, and it was hard for Lavarack not to say: *'I told you so'*, when he'd fought so strongly against Blamey's and other men's derision to warn Australians that Britain's 'Singapore Policy' wouldn't provide the security it promised. Everything he'd predicted had proved right, for while The Royal Navy was busy fighting in Europe, the Japanese were flooding over England's foremost stronghold of Singapore; having brought about the biggest British surrender in history.

Now that Australia was in deep crisis, however, Lavarack knew it wasn't the time for petty vendettas. Its troops had already been defeated in Singapore, Java, Ambon, New Ireland and New Britain, while in the process of overrunning the whole of South East Asia, Japan's forces had landed on New Guinea, and as per Pearl Harbour, had launched 188 planes from their aircraft carriers in the Timor Sea and were bombing Australia's northern city of Darwin, along with its pivotal seaport of Broome.

The newspapers were running hot with headlines that pushed the population into a state of panic:

JAPAN'S ASSAULT ON OUR MAINLAND
IS EXPECTED ANY DAY!

"Well, what are we doing to protect ourselves?" those reading the front-page news demanded, given that nothing of this magnitude had happened before and Australia was standing largely defenceless. With most of its soldiers who'd been serving overseas still sailing home, there was only one adequately trained brigade on hand to defend its shores.

Fortunately, the military and political authorities were working frantically behind the scenes to rectify the situation, and at a hastily convened council of war, Rowell was running through the report he had prepared:

"Our 7th Division and part of our 6th are due back soon," he stated to those seated around the conference table. "And in the meantime, six infantry and two cavalry divisions have been mobilised and are undergoing intensive training, albeit with limited equipment and facilities."

He could see their relief as his words sank in, so he continued:

"In addition, we have recalled a number of our senior

commanders from the Middle East to take command of these newly mobilised formations. Thanks to their recent battle experience, they'll come with fresh energy and the skills we need."

Things were swinging into action, but with the writing already on the wall and the numbers stacked against them, every Australian was bucked-up by Blamey being back on board. For better or worse, his was a name they knew, and there was comfort in that. As there was in General MacArthur being appointed Commander-in-Chief of the South West Pacific, because it meant America was here to help and that Australia wasn't alone.

CHAPTER 33

"THERE'S NO WAY we can win without them," Lavarack said. "And that goes for the rest of the world."

This new injection of American troops and technology would do wonders for that war-weary world. By now, both sides fighting for it were worn out, and while the Axis powers were to look on the fresh US ranks with dread and exhaustion, the Allies, when seeing their millions marching to join them, would say with relief:

"At last! Better late than never."

In the meantime, Lavarack had to hand Blamey back the reins, and that was hard to do when he'd had a taste of the top job and was sure that the limitations of Blamey's bloody-mindedness would, one day, work to the detriment and disrespect of his troops. For while it was Blamey's responsibility to work with the Supreme Commander of the South West Pacific, his greater duty of care was to his fellow countrymen fighting in it. Yet most of them, at the end of the day, would say that he let them down.

For now, however, it seemed that Blamey had done the right thing by giving Lavarack command of The Australian First

Army. It would have come as ample compensation had Blamey not, at the same time, appointed Rowell as Commander of the Australian 1 Corps, responsible for the frontline operations of multiple divisions. That was a real feather in Rowell's cap, yet despite being a role less senior than Lavarack's, it was one for which the latter, with his hardened combat experience, was far better suited.

While it was just one more way for Blamey to clip Lavarack's wings, it was, nonetheless, a big-time gesture on his part where Rowell was concerned, being as much to say: *'No hard feelings'*, after they had ended on such bad terms in Greece.

Rowell was flattered to be given his first field command since his short, Light Horse stint at Gallipoli. But Blamey's bid to win back his allegiance didn't stop there, for this promotion made Rowell the first Duntroon man to command a corps and to reach the rank of lieutenant general. Most men would have been grateful for that, but Rowell wasn't so easily won over, and having witnessed all of which Blamey and his ego were capable, still wanted to reserve his opinion.

At long last, Lavarack wasn't standing alone on Blamey's wrong side; and that was good to know when it was a dangerous place to be.

–oOo–

MacArthur and Blamey had descended on Australia in March, 1942 like Olympian Gods of War, both meeting their match as men of equal arrogance, but with MacArthur having the edge, because he was backed by a more a powerful nation. The best Blamey could do to keep pace was to quickly set up his Allied Land Headquarters in Melbourne, but when MacArthur opted to base his own General Headquarters in Brisbane, Blamey moved fast to do the same.

There, he had done a big reshuffle of his higher command, having Lavarack head up Australia's First Army and Lieutenant General Ivan Mackay, its Second. In his new role, Lavarack was to defend Queensland and New South Wales, which although being imperative at the time, would later see him effectively side-lined to suffer two years of confinement in his own country, with Blamey constantly overlooking him when Australia was in dire need of strong, battle-ready commanders to take over in New Guinea.

At this point, however, it was a plum post, and with Australia in peril and Lavarack set to defend it, he felt it was the prime time to ask Blamey a favour.

"What's the chance of me being promoted to Full General when I take on this role?"

It was a fair request and well and truly Lavarack's due, but Blamey's bounty didn't stretch that far, and without even bothering to confer with Canberra, he answered:

"Unfortunately, on this issue, the government is not willing to commit itself."

To put the onus on the Prime Minister was Blamey's easy way out, and not in a position to contest it, Lavarack's only recourse was to vent his rage in writing:

> *Apparently I am to be cast in the pool of all new promotions. Such is fate with watchful jealousy ever on the lookout above me. There is no generosity in Blamey.*

In one seemingly magnanimous move, Blamey had robbed him of his chance to make his mark. Giving him all the military trappings, but denying him the battlefields beyond overseeing their supply lines.

Lavarack didn't hesitate, however, to congratulate Rowell. They had always been friends, so it wasn't hard to do, and he'd learnt from experience that rather than resent a situation it was always better to embrace it.

"If I can be of any help, just let me know," he said as he shook Rowell's hand, but he had to admit that his best wishes were tinged with envy, for Rowell, now as Commander of New Guinea Force, was setting off for Port Moresby – the hotspot of the war and the prize the Japanese wanted most, because it was the key to controlling the sea lanes of the entire South Pacific.

So far, Major General Basil Morris had been running the show there and was surprised when he was replaced. The only warning he'd had that Rowell was on his way was in a message from Blamey's new Deputy Chief of the General Staff, Major General Vasey.

It simply said:

"Syd is coming."

CHAPTER 34

AS SEASONED OFFICERS, who had been in the Middle East, Rowell and his staff were expected to bring to New Guinea the skill and organisation that Morris and his men, despite doing their best, couldn't provide. When Rowell arrived at the port, he was full of vim and vigour, but with his staff lagging a week behind, Blamey was worried and wired him:

> *This won't do! You must get base staff faster than that. You're running a tactical headquarters now and will need all the help you can get to cope with its urgent, administrative problems.*

Rowell, being a skilled administrator himself, took exception to Blamey's tone and knocked back his suggestion. It was one, however, that like Blamey's sharp mind, shouldn't have been discounted, for Rowell soon found out what an enormous task lay before him. With only a few maps at their disposal, he and his crew were virtually working blind, while the plane carrying their supplies had been shot down by the Japanese and couldn't be located on Papua New Guinea's Kokoda Trail.

The primitive 100km track wound through the island's Owen Stanley Range, and regardless of its steep muddy paths, dense jungle and intolerable weather, was the route the Japanese had chosen to advance on Ports Moresby. It was therefore of prime importance and had to be defended, but like the plane that had gone missing beneath its thick, tropical canopy, Australian troops were feeling just as lost as they macheted their way through the foreign wilderness, fighting a four-month battle of unrelenting suffering and savagery.

They called it the arsehole of the world where those who weren't trained for guerilla warfare, or didn't learn fast, died sooner. In its hellish humidity, small groups of men, infinitely smaller than the mountains surrounding them, were struggling to survive, killing by stealth rather than fighting by the book on open battlefields. Those who conquered the wilderness and its cruelty coped best by quietly bayoneting and slitting enemy throats, while the men among them who couldn't come at the idea were lying down in their droves to die from disease in the midst of the great loneliness.[37]

The only benefit of the god-awful place was that it affected both sides with its bacteria-ridden environment wiping out Allied and Axis powers alike, if not by sickness, then via starvation and extreme exhaustion.

It was a baptism by fire for the young, inexperienced men of Australia's 39th Battalion, who had been rushed there in the emergency to stall the Japanese until better reinforcements arrived. The promise of those better soldiers coming gave the 39th hope, but the hours before that sturdier 2/14 Battalion turned up were to be longest of their lives. Until then, they would be working on a wing and a prayer, because their commander, Lieutenant Colonel Bill Owen,[38] had been killed in action, and all they had in their favour was knowing that his replacement, Lieutenant Colonel Ralph Honner, was on his way.

"He'd better be worth the wait," one soldier said scathingly, for they were still mourning Owen's loss, and having come to rely on him, were sure that no newcomer could measure up.

The fact that this bloke, Honner, was nothing but a teacher and solicitor back home didn't exactly fill them with confidence, but they were soon to find out, that when under fire, he was a most remarkable man. One, who in Greece and Crete, had led his former troops through a series of fighting withdrawals against the numerically superior Germans, and was, according to his military seniors: "*The best company commander in both this and the last Great War.*"

–oOo–

Now that he was in New Guinea, nothing had changed:

"Most of these boys are barely out of their teens," Honner said when he first laid eyes on the 39th's sea of young faces already scarred by the strain of suffering.

Yet, while his was the voice of sympathy, the rest of the regular army didn't view it the same way.

"Bloody Chocos!" they labeled the newly initiated battalion, for like the block of confectionery, their sweet, untried ranks were expected to melt away in the heat of battle.

It was an insult that gave the young men of the 39th a better boost than the malaria shot they'd had in arm, goading them to stage a strong offensive of their own at the Battle of Isurava.

Right from the start, they knew they couldn't win, but with their new '*We'll show 'em*' way of thinking they went about achieving victory in a different way. Slowly but surely, under

Honner's skilled guidance, fighting a controlled retreat, which would not only stem the enemy tide and help save Port Moresby, but would ultimately stop the waves of Japanese invaders from ever breaking loose on Australian shores.

The village of Isurava hardly seemed worth fighting for, propped up high on the Ranges with a dense jungle on one side and steep descent on the other. However, it was a pivotal part of the Kokoda Campaign, and it was among its grass huts that the men of the 39th were told to make their stand. Albeit one, tragically ill-equipped with no more than bayoneted rifles in their hands, bully beef in their bags and the limitations of metal helmets that in the blazing heat slid round like liquid mercury on their heads.

When the blistering sun rose on the morning of August 26, Honner only had time to say a short, silent prayer before the enemy showed itself with the might of its far greater numbers and weaponry.

"Here they come!" he said to his second-in-command, Captain Harry Smith.

And both men braced themselves for the first of many fierce, frontal attacks on their vastly out-numbered Australian position, just as had the British, 63 years before, when facing the Zulus at the famed Rorke's Drift.

In line with the Zulu's 'buffalo-horn' tactic, the Japanese were coming at them from three sides, with their 1/144 Regiment attacking the Australian centre, and their 2/144 and 3/144, respectively, targeting their right and left flanks. They had the Australians surrounded and set to be slaughtered, which made it all the more frustrating for the Japanese when that small band of soldiers refused to go down.

"I don't know how they're doing it," Honner admitted to

Smith midway through the killing spree, for against all odds his boys were answering every enemy attack with swift, savage counterattacks in a show of courage and resilience which went way beyond any commander's expectation.

"They're doing it because they have to," Smith answered without emotion, as he wiped the blood from the flesh wound he, himself, had sustained when leading the last charge.

As a commando, Smith took such brutality in his stride, but even he, like Honner, was astounded by the hardiness and resolve of these young troops under their command. The Japanese, in their desperate bid to find the weak spot in their lines, were hitting them hard with everything they had, while for the sake of their fallen mates, those of the Australians still alive were doubly desperate to defend it.

If one man went down, another would stand in his place, which was a wonder in itself, when even before the battle began, half of them were near dead on their feet from dysentery and every other kind of disease. But whether they had to walk or crawl, they made it to the front line.

By the time the 2/14 Battalion arrived to relieve them, 111 men from the 39th were wounded and 99 were dead.

"Nice to see you," one from its decimated lines said sarcastically to the 2/14's commander, Lieutenant Colonel Albert Key, who might have taken exception had he been able to make out the man's rank.

As it was, the soldier standing before him was caked in mud and blood, and with his skin and uniform coloured the same, Key could only focus on his electric, blue eyes shining in contrast to reply:

"Looks like you boys have done your dash and need a damn good rest."

The battle, unfortunately, was far from finished, and although the men of 2/14 were more experienced, their potential to make a difference had been seriously undermined by their torturous march along the Kokoda Trail. They'd done it at double the pace to make it in time, but having achieved their objective, their exhaustion was showing in their faces drained white with heat and khaki uniforms drenched in sweat.

Having arrived in such a sorry state, they were hoping that the worst of their trials were over, so the now wiser 39th didn't have the heart to tell their reinforcements that they had an even harder slog ahead. Instead, Honner turned with weary resolve to those severely depleted troops of his 39th, and though knowing that they were in dire need of rest themselves said:

"Well boys ... what do you think? You've every right to be relieved, but do we stay to help them out or do we go?"

Perhaps they were too tired to answer, but their silence said it all, when they remained resolutely in place.

Their sticking by the 2/14, unfortunately, didn't win the battle, but for both battalions, it was to be remembered as a profound example of courage and sacrifice by the young Australian soldiers, who fought under terrible conditions to protect their country. What had been the 39th's initial ranks of a thousand men had already been reduced to 470 before the battle had even begun, but by its end, that number had been whittled down to just 147. Yet, between the two brave battalions, only one man from the 2/14 would be posthumously awarded the Victoria Cross for conspicuous valour.[39]

As far as Honner was concerned, every last one of them deserved it, and he said as much in his speech to those of his 39th who survived:

Now I don't know all of you by name, but I feel that I know every one of you well, for we met and fought together at Isurava. By fighting for the track you have helped save your nation, while your courage and fortitude have been an inspiration. You have seen things in this place that no man should witness. Things you must forget, but for which history will remember you. I want you to know that you are the finest soldiers I have ever seen, and that I am honoured to be your brother.[40]

CHAPTER 35

PEARL HARBOUR and General MacArthur's escape by PT Boat from the Philippines to Australia had undermined America, but their recent wins at the Battles of Coral Sea and Midway had changed all that. Now, with those US victories under his belt and his own not-so-perfect performance behind him, MacArthur was standing tall and being highly critical of what he said was Australia's poor showing in New Guinea.

"Its troops aren't living up to expectation and have proved no match for the enemy in jungle warfare," he communicated to the Chief of Staff of the United States Army, General George Marshall.

"Well if that's the case," Marshall replied. "Don't tell me. Tell the man at the top."

In this instance, he wasn't referring to President Roosevelt, but to the man it more directly concerned, Australia's Prime Minister John Curtin.

Immediately, MacArthur put through a call to the country's capital:

"What they need up there," he said to Curtin over the secraphone. "Is the aggressive leadership that's sadly lacking."

Judging by the volume of his voice and its dictatorial tone, he may as well have been thumping his fist on Curtin's parliamentary desk, and not taking to it too kindly, Curtin replied with measured calm.

"Who exactly do you have in mind?"

"Your Commander-in-Chief, Blamey, of course."

Curtin hesitated, for the situation among members of the Australian military hierarchy was tenuous. Since Blamey's less than commendable actions in Greece, his credibility with his peers and troops had been in question, while Curtin, himself, still wasn't entirely sure that he respected him. He had no idea that Blamey, in return, had nothing but the highest regard for him, and would never say or hear a word said against him.

That was because Blamey knew a gentleman when he saw one, and seeing as much in Curtin, didn't resent him speaking what he believed to be the truth, even if that truth wasn't in his favour:

"I have grave doubts about Blamey's moral fibre," Curtin was sorry to admit.

And at this admission, MacArthur sighed with frustration before answering:

"Look, Prime Minister, your problem is simple. You must decide whether you are fighting a war or running a scripture class. If it's a scripture class, then get rid of Blamey as quickly as you can. But if you want to put your utmost into winning the war, hold him with everything you have. I can assure you that you have not, in your country, another man who is even nearly comparable to him."

"That's certainly debatable," Curtin flashed back on behalf of the host of fine officers Australia had on hand.

MacArthur, however, seemed convinced that Blamey was the best of them, and so in his ignorance of military matters, Curtin gave the go-ahead for Blamey to take control in New

Guinea, while those more cynical in political circles suggested that MacArthur, rather than paying Blamey a compliment, was setting him up as a scapegoat.

Blamey's in-house enemies couldn't have been more pleased, while one member of the Australian War Cabinet was happy to say it straight:

"Moresby is going to fall. Send Blamey up there and let him fall with it!"[41]

The worst of it was that Blamey, as shrewd as ever, suspected that they'd got it right.

"I"m leaving for New Guinea in a few days," he told his friend, Major General Sam Burston, who as the Director-General of Medical Services, had the vast responsibility of seeing to the health and welfare of Australian soldiers in every theatre of the war.

"Why?" he asked with concern. "Are things really that bad up there?"

"No, but Canberra's lost it! Both Curtin and MacArthur want me to go to Moresby, and believe me, it wasn't a request, but a direct order. I remember what happened to 'The Auk' in the desert, so it's best that I just keep my mouth shut and go!"

He was harking back to British Field Marshal Claude Auchinleck, who despite winning with his 8th Army against Rommel at El Alamein, had soon after been relieved of duty for daring to disagree with Churchill over the Northern Front strategies.

It was a sorry fate for a soldier riding high on success, and one which Blamey had to avoid at all costs considering that, so far, he hadn't seen such success and was being put in command of another campaign that had 'failure' written all over it.

CHAPTER 36

HONNER'S 39TH BATTALION, being on its last legs, was withdrawn from the Battle of Brigade Hill. As the next in the series of fierce engagements to stop the Japanese advance, fresher troops from Brigadier Arnold Potts' 21st Brigade had taken over, while for the first time, the Americans were fighting at their side. Primarily, playing their part with air support and thc odd bomb strike, while aiding as runners and stretcher-bearers for the more experienced Australian troops, who were still expected to bear the brunt of the campaign.

The Japanese were coming at them again, but this time with a ruthless brutality based on their commander, Colonel Masao Kurunose's single-minded determination to get the Australians who had refused to die at Isurava.

He was sticking to the same flanking manoeuvre, but doing it to better effect with his overwhelming number of troops cutting off three Australian battalions and forcing them to retreat after making many costly counter-attacks. By then, 87 Australians were dead and 77 wounded, while 500 others had been lost from exhaustion while carrying the wounded on their merciless jungle march to avoid encirclement. It was their only way out and they had to keep moving, because the Japanese, at this point, hadn't been taking prisoners and weren't averse to the occasional beheading.

The battle was a severe setback for the Allied forces with high casualties on both sides. Every Australian who fell took twice as many enemy troops down with him. Yet, the best that could be said of what had been the most savage encounter of the campaign was that it gained crucial time for the Allies, which went towards their eventual victory on the Kokoda Trail.

The conditions had been so appalling that the history books would compare it to WWI's Dardanelles, with those who didn't die from disease, fatigue or starvation, going down by way of bayonets, machine guns, grenades and every other vile means.

"So don't tell us about our boys at Gallipoli," WWII's Brigade Hill battalions would say. "For now we've had our fair share of what they suffered."

–oOo–

It wasn't long after this terrible stage in the campaign that Blamey was due to arrive in New Guinea. His mandate from MacArthur was to 'energize the situation', and to that end, The Supreme Commander had written him a curt note:

The performance of your troops in New Guinea is not nearly good enough. It's up to you to do something about it.

Blamey had already done something about it by sending a note to Rowell, in which he explained, as tactfully as possible, why he was coming to take over.

> *The powers-that-be have determined that I shall myself go to New Guinea for a while and operate from there. I hope you will not be upset at this decision, and will not think that it implies any lack of confidence in yourself. It arises out of the fact that we have very inexperienced politicians who are inclined to panic on every possible occasion, and I believe that the relationship between us, personally, is such that we can make the arrangement work without any difficulty.*

He'd signed off in the hope that Rowell would take it well, but in fact, he took it very badly, because the timing was so strategic on Blamey's part. Certainly, while their Australian troops had been on the back foot, Rowell hadn't expected praise for the hard work he'd been doing behind the scenes, but since Brigade Hill, there'd been the Battle of Milne Bay that had turned the tide in their favour, and he was sure that Blamey was coming on cue to take the credit.

It was only fortunate for Rowell that he was still in command of 1 Corps and privy to all top level military discussions. But bit by bit, his 'talking terms' with Blamey was breaking down to personal insults and bouts of bad temper, and with Rowell being aggrieved and speaking his mind so often, Blamey was fed up ... fed up enough to pay Rowell a backhanded compliment, before undermining him in the report he wrote to the Australian Prime Minister:

> *Rowell has very great ability; is quick in decision and sound in judgment. There can be no question of his personal courage, but he lacks the reserves*

> *of nervous energy over a period of long strain. I found him difficult during the last few days in Greece, and as his commander, had to exercise considerable tact, which is the reverse of what it should be.*

Having started the note by saying something nice, Blamey knew that Curtin would construe the rest of his words as being fair. None of them, however, explained exactly why Rowell had been 'difficult during the last few days in Greece', or that it had been due to his dismay and ongoing disrespect for Blamey who'd so abruptly deserted his troops.

For his part, Rowell had written a letter of his own to Lavarack.[42] Not as an appeal for help, but simply to use him as a sounding board:

> *The plain fact is that Blamey hasn't enough moral courage to fight the Cabinet on the issue of confidence in me. If they have none, then I'll willingly be pulled out, but what angers me most is that Blamey comes here when our fortunes have changed and all is likely to be well. He cannot influence the local situation in any way, but he will get the kudos and it will be said, rather pityingly, that he came here to hold my hand and bolster me up.*

Lavarack read what he had to say and felt sympathetic, for now that Rowell had rubbed Blamey the wrong way, he hadn't a hope in hell of winning. With that in mind, he wrote back a friendly warning:

> *Tread carefully. I've learnt from firsthand experience that Blamey can't be beaten. And somehow, I've come to respect him for that.*

His note would have come as some solace, had Rowell not, soon after, suffered another blow to his pride.

–oOo–

"May I suggest that you fly to Milne Bay," MacArthur said to Blamey. "And order your Major General Clowes in command there to send a force by air to Wanigela."

It was an important step forward, and there was nothing wrong with MacArthur having initiated it, other than the fact that Rowell had been totally left out of the loop.

"I'm not even being consulted on anything anymore!" he stormed into Blamey's office to say. 'It's bad enough that you've bypassed me and have done nothing to safeguard my interests, but I draw the line at you and MacArthur making me eat dirt!"

Their relations had hit rock bottom, and rather than answer, Blamey sat in stony silence as Rowell raged from the room. Now that all pretence between them was gone, Blamey struck the final blow in his weekly report to Curtin:

> *Rowell has proved most difficult and recalcitrant and considers himself very unjustly used. I have permitted him to state his case, which he has done with greatfrankness directly against me. His reluctance to provide logistical information has left me having to search for details myself and there is a definite atmosphere of obstruction.*

He signed off having sealed his former friend's fate, and within days, Rowell was relieved of duty and recalled to Australia. That should have been enough to satisfy Blamey, but he'd gone on to make a further suggestion in his report's postscript:

> *Perhaps we should send Rowell to the Middle East. His rank, of course, will have to be reduced to major general, so that he's junior to Lieutenant General Morshead over there.*

Unaware of those demeaning words, Rowell had decided to stop off in Brisbane to state his case to MacArthur. But the big man had already been briefed on the situation, and being on Blamey's side, wasn't the least bit won over.

"Your attitude to a superior officer in a theatre of active operations is quite unpardonable," he scolded. "I can only hope, for your sake, Rowell, that there won't be an enquiry into the matter. I, for one, will never agree to you being given command again."

The interview was short and insulting and Rowell walked from it feeling shell-shocked.

Yet what Curtin had to say when he arrived in Canberra was even worse.

"It was wrong for you to find fault with Blamey," he said more sanctimoniously than had MacArthur. "He was sent to New Guinea against his will and on my orders, even though he expressed his fullest confidence in his commanders there."

Rowell left the meeting shaking his head in wonderment over Blamey having, once again, smooth-talked his way back into everyone's good graces.

How quickly people forget, he thought as he walked down the corridors of Parliament House.

For only a few months before, Blamey had been accused of being a coward. Yet, for having stood by his men, he – Rowell, was being made to feel like filth, while Blamey had come out smelling of roses.

CHAPTER 37

"THE MAN DESERVES A MEDAL for bringing other men down," Lavarack said of Blamey.

He had heard what happened to Rowell and was almost as bitter on his behalf as he was on his own.

Blamey's big reshuffle of ranks in New Guinea had seen Lieutenant General Edmund Herring replace Rowell, Brigadier Ivan Dougherty take over Potts' 21st Brigade, while Major General 'Tubby' Allen's command of the 7th Division had gone to Major General Vasey.

"The first duty of a solider is obedience to his superiors," MacArthur said to those new commanders coming on board, making blatant reference to Rowell in his show of support for Blamey.

Meanwhile, Allen, who'd been in charge of operations along the Kokoda Trail, had been treated just as brutally for having moved too slowly, MacArthur and Blamey believed, in pursuit of the enemy across the Owen Stanley Range.

"But that's not fair!" Allen's men said in his and their own defence, when they'd done their level best under appalling conditions and it was for Allen, alone, that they'd been prepared to lay down their lives.

Allen, himself, was every bit as offended and surprised, but as always, took the high road.

"Well, if I have to hand over my command," he said with self-restraint, "then I'm glad it's to Vasey, because his rough-edged ways make him every bit as popular with his troops."

It had been a huge shake up to facilitate what MacArthur and Blamey saw as the leadership of stronger men. Yet in all its reconfiguring, Lavarack's name hadn't even been in the running.

He was stunned considering how hard he'd been campaigning to have his First Army Headquarters moved to New Guinea. Most senior officers agreed that sending him and his staff there was the sensible thing to do, but for personal reasons, and at the cost of his country's welfare, Blamey refused to let them go.

Lavarack had no doubt, now, that Blamey loathed him, and his having treated him so badly made the feeling mutual. Still, however, as a dedicated military man, Lavarack stood by his senior officer in every way, down to having leapt to his defence when, during a recent strategy meeting, MacArthur objected to Blamey giving him advice and said:

Don't teach your grandmother to suck eggs!

Unfortunately for Lavarack, Blamey was never to show loyalty of the like to him, despite knowing how willing and ready Lavarack was to play a more active role in the war. Since the Battles of Coral Sea and Midway had removed the imminent threat to Australia's mainland, its First Army's responsibility of protecting it had lessened and Lavarack had been hoping for some sort of hands-on command in the combat zone.

"I'm all but redundant here and could be so much more

effective in New Guinea," he'd said to Blamey back in August. "I could really help Rowell out by having my First Army Headquarters moved there?"

Blamey's reply came back clipped and barely considered.

"The troops in New Guinea comprise a 'task force', not an army."

Obscure as that answer was, it was meant as a definite 'no', but Lavarack wasn't about to give up.

His having asked the question at all, however, was a big mistake. For ever since, Blamey had been blocking any chance of him taking on any such role and was chipping away at what was left of his First Army command in Australia; day by day, pilfering the best of his staff officers for posts in New Guinea, while leaving Lavarack, himself, behind.

It was plain to see what Blamey was doing, but being, as always, dutiful to his senior officer, Lavarack could only vent his rage in his diary:

The way it's going, I envisage a gradual reduction of my First Army to vanishing point.

This was the reality that had him make his second mistake by broaching the subject with MacArthur. But Blamey, having anticipated as much, beat him to the punch and by the time it was Lavarack's turn to speak the American Supreme Commander had already been talked round to Blamey's way of thinking.

Everything, from that point, went downhill fast with Blamey convinced that Lavarack was scheming against him.

–oOo–

"I take a poor view of you dining out with Keith Murdoch,"[43] he lashed out the second Lavarack walked into his office.

It wasn't like Blamey to lose control in front of his staff officers, but where Australian newspaper magnate Murdoch was concerned, he always saw red. Since they'd first met, Murdoch had made no bones about the fact that he disliked him, and with his top level connections and the power of his mighty press, had come close to ruining Blamey's career back in his controversial Police Commissioner days. He'd failed, but Murdoch wasn't a man who liked losing, and because he had also disapproved of Blamey's questionable performance in Greece, it seemed certain that he was now working doubly hard to have him removed as Commander-in-Chief.

Murdoch, for Blamey, meant bad news, and beyond the pun, was a man he viewed with the utmost suspicion, as he did any military officer who socialised with him.

"I'm afraid you've been misinformed, sir. I wasn't with Murdoch last night," Lavarack answered, albeit annoyed at having to account for himself in this way. "Yes, I know him and have dined with him before, but in this instance, it's a case of mistaken identity."

"Don't give me that! You were seen sitting at his table."

At this bald allegation, Lavarack drew a sharp breath.

"I can accept, sir, that you've made a mistake, but I will never accept being called a liar," he then snapped, before striding from the room without being dismissed.

Blamey waited until he'd slammed the door and then said to his Aide-de-Camp, Captain Norman Carlyon:

"I know the bastards are talking behind my back."

"I'm sorry, sir, but I'm with Lavarack on this," Carlyon surprised him by replying. "Why would he bother speaking behind your back when he's never stinted at saying exactly what he thinks straight to your face?"

Much as he hated to admit it, Blamey knew that Carlyon was right – that Lavarack was too strong and morally upstanding to indulge in disloyalty of the like. Yet, his associating with Murdoch at all was a red rag to a bull, and as far as Blamey was concerned, put paid to any chance Lavarack had of going to New Guinea, as had Rowell's prior attempts to get him there.

–oOo–

"If it were up to me, I'd get Lavarack here post-haste," Rowell had said to Blamey not long before he was sacked. "Our New Guinea Force is getting too big to handle with the limited resources at my disposal. If Lavarack's HQ was here in charge of ops, it would really help and you wouldn't be burdened by having to come yourself."

Blamey, at the time, had glared back at him as if looks could kill.

"You know the reason why I can't do that," he'd snapped. "It'd mean bringing in a commander I don't like and don't want."

"Deplorable!" Lavarack was later to say when he found out. "And what a crime that Rowell was sacrificed to that very unworthy god."

CHAPTER 38

WHEN LAVARACK MADE A FLEETING VISIT to New Guinea in October, Blamey's greeting was icy. They hadn't seen eye to eye in regard to Rowell's dismissal, yet though the subject was still raw, it was open for discussion over dinner.

"I will never again entertain any esteem for Rowell," Blamey stated categorically before forking in a mouthful of potato and peas. "Do you know that he actually accused me of lying about the government's request that I come to New Guinea?"

Blamey was rightfully angry about that, but not nearly as angry as he was about Lavarack having come as well. Their awkward silence during dessert made that clear, so Lavarack skipped the post-meal glass of port, and excusing himself from the table went back to barracks to write in his diary:

> *I am certain now of Blamey's open hostility towards me. Rowell was doing excellent work here in Port Moresby, and since his sacking, there's been an atmosphere of unease and suspicion. When I hear Blamey speak of others who've displeased him, I can only wonder what stories he's told of me.*

It was clear that Blamey was under stress. Everyone could see it in his physical state and fits of nervous hiccupping that had strangely kicked in the second Lavarack arrived. The man obviously had a bad effect on him, but that was something that Blamey had decided to fix, once and for all, when Lavarack left on his inspection tour of Milne Bay.

"I intend to return to Australia in the early hours of November 1," Lavarack informed him before setting out on Friday, October 30.

When he returned to Port Moresby later that afternoon, however, he was surprised to find that Blamey had moved his departure for Australia forward a day.

"Are you that keen to get rid of me?" he asked in part jest.

"Not at all," Blamey answered without humour. "I'm merely saving you from yourself, because Canberra's complaining about you being away from HQ too often. Apart from your unnecessary trip here, you've apparently visited Melbourne an excessive four times in three months."

At this degrading reprimand, Lavarack's body seized with rage.

"I consider myself best judge of my needs to make visits," he fired back without monitoring his savage tone to his senior officer. "And it's been three visits in four months, the first two of which were ordered by you. I'd like to see this so-called complaint from Canberra."

"I haven't got it on me," Blamey barked back. "But either way, there was no need for you to come here."

"None other than MacArthur insisting that all senior officers see the conditions in New Guinea for themselves. What do you think ... that I'm here on a joyride!"

Blamey, at this point, put an end to the argument.

"Well let's just say that I am here at our government's request, and that while I am, there's no scope for you."

That left Lavarack no option but to return to his exile in Queensland, dazed to a degree, by what had been a most demoralising experience. The treatment of him had gone beyond bad, and when Blamey had topped it off by allocating him sub-standard accommodation in a rusty, tin shed, it had been the last straw.

A firm line had been drawn in the sand, but Blamey wasn't to stop there. For little by little, he was bleeding Lavarack's First Army dry, with what was left of its command structure being fast eroded away.

"Every time he calls me to his office, I'm expecting him to tell me that my army's being disbanded," Lavarack said to his second-in-command, Major General Frank Berryman.

Lavarack's concern over the matter had him set up his First Army's Signal School to replace personnel already sent to New Guinea. It was the best way to safeguard his own position, but he should have known that Blamey wouldn't let him get away with that.

"You've done some fine work there," Blamey complimented him. "It seems your Signal School students are ready for transfer faster than expected. I want you to get them off to New Guinea as soon as possible, along with the rest of your officers."

No amount of cursing under his breath could make Lavarack feel better about having to comply, but he hadn't expected it to go a step further when Blamey was called to Canberra for an important meeting with the Prime Minister.

–oOo–

"If you should fall ill or become a casualty of war, we must know who is to be your successor," Curtin put to him as a dispassionate politician. "We, here in Canberra, assume that, as the next senior officer in line, it will be Lieutenant General John Lavarack."

"It certainly won't be!" Blamey shot back as if on the warpath, but when he saw the stunned look on the Prime Minister's face, he called off the charge.

"Look," he then continued in a more reasonable way. "There are many reasons why I haven't put Lavarack in charge of operations in New Guinea. The most important of which is that he doesn't possess the attributes of a first class commander."

"Well, I must say I'm surprised," Curtin answered. "He's always struck me as being a man of strong mind and purpose who doesn't hesitate to ram his point home. The very definition, I would have thought, of a true commander."

Blamey, however, as the military expert, wasn't prepared to listen and wiped the Prime Minister's point of view aside.

"I'm sure," he continued, pursuing his own, "that after some further experience in higher command, Lieutenant General Leslie Morshead will be better suited for the role."

In one fell swoop, Blamey had put a cap on Lavarack's military career, and for that Lavarack would never forgive him.

One day, no doubt, Blamey will do himself in the eye, Lavarack could only content himself by thinking.

And in fulfillment of the wish, Blamey came close to doing just that, when after the Battle of Ioribaiwa, he made the fatal mistake of calling his own men cowards.

CHAPTER 39

"THE JAPS BLEW THEIR HEADS CLEAN OFF!" Sergeant Eric Williams reported back to his 2/16 Battalion on the day the battle began.

He was in a state of shock after what he'd seen, with his eyes flashing wild and words spitting like machine-gun fire from his mouth.

He'd been one in a scouting party of five that had been caught in the jungle crossfire, and pinned down by a Japanese mountain gun barrage, three of the men sought protection behind a tree with their heads pressed tight to its trunk.

"*Jesus Christ!*" Williams let out when the percussion of a shell exploding in the treetop above them split their skulls wide open.

His captain, albeit with head still attached, was lying lifeless beside him, so Williams scrambled to his feet, and with a fleeting bit of clear-thinking through the carnage, grabbed his mates' grenades and took the bolts from their rifles.

"I'll be buggered if I'm going to let those Jap bastards get their hands on these," he said, as he slung them into his kit and got the hell out of there.

"What about Captain Grayden?" an officer from Williams' battalion asked.

"Dead!" Williams answered without emotion "All of them dead ... just like that."

Under the chaotic and brutal conditions of jungle warfare, this latest Battle of Iriobaiwa had been a nightmare, with the Australians, in between making their measured retreat, having to stop for rounds of close-quarters combat; going face-to-face with the enemy, whose fear-based sweat and fetid breath made killing them way too real and personal.

Two Japanese battalions were in hot pursuit of the Australians they'd fought at Brigade Hill, the remnants of which, from 21st Brigade, including Sergeant Williams 2/16 Battalion, had been hastily positioned to defend Ioribaiwa Ridge. Their numbers were severely depleted, and without artillery support to counter that of the Japanese, there'd been little they could do but beat back several enemy probing patrols and kill 30 Japanese soldiers in an ambush at an abandoned food dump.

Meanwhile, most of the men from the brigade had become so numb to the never-ending enemy fire that they were no longer even bothering to take cover. Instead, watching with blank-eyed indifference as the shells rained down around them and their fellow soldiers got shot to pieces.

It was still with a keen sense of survival, however, that Sergeant Williams suddenly looked up in surprise to see a figure staggering through the jungle towards them.

"What the hell!" he said as if he'd seen ghost.

But this ghost was flesh and blood rigged out in khaki uniform, who after taking two faltering steps closer and then falling to his knees, became recognisable as the assumed-dead Captain Bill Grayden.

Instantly, Williams was up and running to his aid.

"I'm so sorry, sir, that I left you for dead, but I could have sworn you were," he gave in rapid explanation, as he secured Grayden's arm around his own shoulder and told him to lean his full weight on him.[44]

Only a few hours later, Grayden had recovered sufficiently to write his report:

> *I remember putting my thumb up against the tree to steady myself when I saw the flash of the enemy's guns 500 yards away. Next thing I knew I was coming to, having been knocked out by the fifteen-inch shell that exploded in the treetop and killed my men.*[45]

He didn't go into detail about the state in which he found those dismembered men, but it sufficed to say that the whole battle was a horror fest and that every man who played a part would never forget it.

"Well at least it's something we can tell our grandchildren," one soldier joked to lighten the mood.

But that wasn't likely when, for the rest of their lives, they'd be incapable of opening their lips to speak of it.

–oOo–

The battle was over before Blamey had even arrived in New Guinea, and at the time, he'd been sorry that it ended in a stalemate. Neither side had lost nor won, but nevertheless, it had stood him in good stead, because as a result of it, as Rowell had predicted, the Australians had finally stopped the Japanese advance by fighting them to a standstill. All of which would go down in the records as Blamey having saved the day.

Despite their Australian casualty count being a few bodies more than the enemy's dead and wounded, the battle had been a crucial, watershed moment in the Kokoda Trail Campaign. The Japanese had exhausted their supply line, and with them being as close as they'd ever get to Port Moresby, the wheels of war had turned and now the strong, victorious Allied counter-offensive began.

It was a formidable achievement for which those who'd fought expected high praise, but Blamey didn't see it the same way.

CHAPTER 40

"I'M SICK TO DEATH of the word retreat," he said two weeks later when addressing the men of the 21st Brigade on an army ground near Port Moresby.[46]

He was referring to Brigadier Kenneth Eather, who while in overall command of the forces at Ioribaiwa, had overestimated the strength of the enemy and decided to withdraw his 25th Brigade fighting in support of the 21st. He had sent that brigade to make a stand at Imita Ridge, which proved a successful manoeuvre, but at the time it looked like defeat and Allied Headquarters hadn't been happy.

"No soldier should be afraid to fight and die," Blamey went on, raising his right fist.

"But you were nearly beaten by an inferior force and Australian troops should be better than that. You must remember that it's the rabbit who runs who gets shot, not the man holding the gun."

As Blamey's ADC, Major Carlyon was standing to attention at his side, and while not flinching at his words, couldn't believe that their Commander-in-Chief had just called his men cowards.

Nor could his troops, and a wave of angry murmurs washed over their ranks. After the hell they'd been through, they'd expected a pat on the back – not a slap in the face!

"Well why don't you go and fight yourself, you fat bastard!" one soldier said, loud enough for those around him to smirk, but not within earshot of the officers to whom his comment would have meant a court-martial.

None of the officers, in fact, noticed, because they were too busy trying to settle their troops. All of them worried that, after such an insult, Blamey would be lucky to escape with his life. By the time they managed to bring them under control, the only way the men could show their contempt was by disobeying the 'eyes-right' order in Blamey's direction when they were told to carry out their march-past parade.

The mood was one of fury, as was that of General Potts, who as the brigade's former commander, was seething with rage.

"I swear to fry Blamey's soul in the afterlife over this incident," he hissed under his breath as he watched the men of his old 21st go by.

For quite apart from their severely depleted numbers, any fool could see what they'd sacrificed and suffered. To even suggest that such men had run like rabbits was outrageous, and Blamey, seeing the reaction he was getting all round, now realised it.

"I didn't intend to offend them," he said in what looked like genuine concern. "I just wanted to steel them for future battles and to buoy them up from being the very best to something even better."

The damage, however, had been done and every Australian was incensed when they heard the news. While Blamey had always had a knack of talking his way out of any sticky situation, this time he'd gone too far and made a mistake that wouldn't be forgiven or forgotten. For the first time in his life he was floundering and had a lot of work to do to make amends.

CHAPTER 41

HE STARTED BY VISITING his wounded soldiers in hospital, but that didn't work with those who weren't in the process of dying whistling him out of the ward with a round of the hit song *'Run Rabbit Run"*.

It seemed he had to do something more spectacular to win back their allegiance, so he did it by speaking up on their behalf at the Battle of Buna-Gona.

–oOo–

"Frankly, I'd rather send in more Australians, because I know they'll fight," he said to MacArthur, whose much-lauded American troops had just proved so disappointing.

While it gave Blamey great satisfaction to say it and lifted him a little in his own men's estimation, it was a bitter pill for MacArthur to swallow when he had been so scathing about Australian soldiers in the past and now had to admit that they measured up better than his own.

"It's all my fault," MacArthur said, but only to himself, because it had been for political rather than strategic reasons that he'd pushed his unprepared troops so hard for quick results.

He had underestimated the fanatical defences of the Japanese forces at the New Guinea beachheads of Buna, Gona and Sananada, and sent in his ill-equipped 32nd Infantry Division to tackle what was a hellhole of deprivation and deplorable jungle conditions. It was something the Australians had been facing for so long that they'd become hardened to it, but for the 'fresh-to-the-scene' Americans who'd been thrust into the fray too fast, it was a fiasco. They hadn't been trained for such vicious, guerilla warfare, and with their critical lack of food, ammunition and defence against disease, the enemy had it all over them and they went down like flies.

Their series of embarrassing battle reverses had come as a blow, and while their poor performance was drawing criticism from all sides, the Australians, though feeling sorry for them, were looking smug and weren't saying a word.

All of it put MacArthur in a very bad mood, and US Lieutenant General Robert Eichelberger had to bear the brunt of it when ordered to assume command of the American troops in New Guinea and fix the problem.

"Take Buna," MacArthur told him. "Or don't come back alive!"

–oOo–

Beyond their friendly rivalry, however, MacArthur and Blamey were working together well, with their combined efforts soon to perform miracles.

Vasey's Australian 7th Division had pushed the Japanese from Kokoda and had pursued them to the coast. While despite the Americans having, so far, put up a poor show there, it was solely due to the stellar victory of their fellow countrymen at Guadalcanal that the enemy had been forced back to that coast's Buna, Gona and Sananand a Beaches.

In the process, America had turned the tide of the Pacific War.

As yet, the Japanese weren't ready to admit it, and like cornered prey preparing to die, were waiting for the fierce, final showdown on what would be New Guinea's blood-soaked sands.

Australia's 18th Brigade, with a squadron of tanks, had been deployed to back up the Americans, while its 21st had gone to relieve the 25th, which while fighting at Gona Beach, had lost so many men that it was in a state of crisis. One from which their 21st reinforcements wouldn't be exempt:

–oOo–

"We want the Australian 2/27 Battalion to make a stand on that hill," came the order from distant command.

So distant that those who made it couldn't clearly see that that hill was completely exposed and that the men of the 2/27 fighting for it would be virtually wiped out in one night. For those of them who survived the slaughter, it was to be a brutal re-run of what had so recently been their fighting retreat from the Battle of Brigade Hill. This time, taking them a month to carry their wounded to safety through the abysmal tropical wilderness.

Their commanding officer, Lieutenant Colonel Geoffrey Cooper, would lead the way with his shrapnel-wounded right arm hanging limp at his side. Yet, with one arm or two, there was nothing he could do to save the many of his men who died en route from exhaustion and disease, and by the time they made it to Port Moresby, only three officers and 67 men of his original 620-strong battalion were left alive.

CHAPTER 42

SUCH SUFFERING MADE IT HARD to believe that the Battle of the Beachheads was to wind up as an Allied win; one which would strip the Japanese of access to Australia and boot them out of New Guinea for good.

Right now, however, the dead and wounded were rolling in from the action raging on the coast, and Blamey, having attended the latest press photo shoot with MacArthur, had decided to drop by the main dressing station at the village of Soputa to see to the welfare of his injured men.

The name of the base sounded impressive, yet it was nothing but a shanty standing on cane stilts with a canvas roof strung between. That, being the best his Australians could do on short notice after their field hospital on the beach was bombed by the Japanese. With no respect for the red cross painted on its roof, their dive-bombers had zeroed in on it killing most of the staff and patients inside, and ever since, all medics relying on the symbol's sense of immunity, had stopped sporting it on their sleeves, because the enemy was using it as target practice.

It made it difficult for those medics to move the few infirmary survivors inland to the relative safety of the jungle where, at the crossroads of the Kokoda-Sananada Trails, they had quickly set up their makeshift facility. It wasn't much to speak of standing without walls in the middle of the wilderness and rain, but it was sufficient to provide shelter for the field hospital's remaining staff, who were doing their best to bandage up the wounded arriving in droves.

Blamey had to pick his way through them to see what was going on within, and feeling himself to be on a mission of mercy was surprised, as was everyone else, when he instantly lost his temper.

"What in the hell's going on here?" he demanded when he saw that the dental surgeon on duty was tending to a Japanese POW rather than looking after his own.

That surgeon, with his controlled, handsome face, looked up in response, and refocusing his eyes from his intense work, stepped aside so that Blamey could see for himself.

"Dear God!" Blamey said in dismay, having to blink back his revulsion at the sight of the patient's jaw, which due to a grenade, was swinging loose on its sinews.

"Enemy or not, sir, no human being should suffer this," the doctor then explained; and Blamey, though thinking it better to put the man out of his misery with a bullet, let him get on with his work.

It was intricate and a wonder to watch, when under primitive conditions, and with only basic tools at his disposal, the doctor was having to operate standing ankle-deep in mud, powering his outdated drilling machine with the constant pumping of its pedal with his foot.

The process was exhausting even for those, who like Blamey, were simply watching on. But the doctor didn't quit until he achieved what appeared to be the impossible by firmly reattaching the man's jaw to his face.

"What's your name?" Blamey asked after it was all over.

And when the doctor answered: 'Smith', he thought it a shame that such an ordinary name should belong to a man who seemed, in every way, so exceptional.

CHAPTER 43

IT WAS ENOUGH to make Blamey want to aspire to greater things, which he may well have done had the matter of Lavarack not been weighing on his mind. Although the Battle of the Beachheads was over, the war was still in full swing and Lavarack was being relentless in his push for a fighting command.

"Which is a complete waste of my time," Blamey thought, when he had no intention of giving him one and was sick to death of keeping up the pretence that he'd ever been considering it. Especially now, when he'd only been back at his Brisbane headquarters for a few, short hours and Lavarack was already at his door.

Nobody could be that fond of war, Blamey was sure, while keeping on the alert for Lavarack's hidden agenda. It never crossed his wary mind that Lavarack was playing it straight and just wanted to be the best he could be as a soldier.

"Why not me?" Lavarack was now asking as he paced the office floor, but with his Commander-in-Chief sitting in his usual intractable silence, he suddenly stopped wearing the carpet thin and slammed his fist down hard on Blamey's desk.

"For God's sake!" he said. "We're fighting a war here with our country in dire need of decent field commanders. What does it matter whether you like me or not?"

It mattered more than he knew, and with Blamey still refusing to say a word, Lavarack strode from the room, unaware that Major Carlyon, who'd been in on the meeting, was watching after him with sympathy of sorts, because he knew that nothing Lavarack could say or do would ever shift Blamey.

"How could it hurt, sir, to give him what he wants?" Carlyon dared ask when Lavarack was out of earshot. "It seems to me that it would be the best way of getting him off your back."

It was a brave man who chose to speak up on Lavarack's behalf and Blamey looked up at him with eyes as cold as ice to give an equally icy answer.

"Carlyon," he said. "The man has command of the First Army with the rank of lieutenant general. What more can he want but my job, which is all that's left?"

Blamey was sure that it was what Lavarack wanted, and fed up with having him forever breathing down his neck, he'd now decided to quash the man's aspirations to that end for good.

–oOo–

His first step was to fly to Canberra to seek sanction for Lavarack's promotion, but in the most backhanded way:

"Lavarack is dissatisfied as GOC First Army," he informed Prime Minister Curtin.

"He's shown this dissatisfaction by being most difficult to work with over the years, and by not cooperating with Generals Morshead and Herring in New Guinea. He is, however, a most capable officer who deserves respect and one, who I believe would benefit from a big change."

That change, with Curtin's say-so, was to be big enough to take Lavarack to the other side of world and well out of Blamey's way.

–oOo–

"I've recommended you for a new position," Blamey later summoned Lavarack to his Brisbane office to say and, at long last, Lavarack's face broke into a broad smile.

"You're to replace Major General Steele as Head of our Australian Military Mission in Washington."

Instantly, the smile fell from Lavarack's face and Blamey feigned surprise.

"I would have thought that such a prestigious post would please you," he said, knowing full well that to relieve such a warrior as Lavarack of his weapons was the cruelest thing he could do.

That smile of Lavarack's was back, but this time being wry, because Blamey had, at long last, won the war between them and Lavarack had no recourse but to walk from the room without saying a word.

To be assigned to Washington was the greatest of accolades, and for having arranged it, Blamey looked like a saint. But it wasn't what Lavarack wanted and he could only hope that the man wouldn't rub it in by coming to see him off.

That, however, Blamey couldn't resist. With entourage in tow, he was waiting at the naval dock that was decked out in bunting red, white and blue, with every piece of military pomp to send Lavarack on his way, bar the embarrassment of a big brass band.

It made it all the more difficult for Lavarack to say goodbye, but with no love lost between them he was surprised when, instead of the customary salute, Blamey reached out to shake his hand.

"Bye Johnny," he said, using a first name familiarity from years past which, if Lavarack didn't know better, could have been construed as warmth.

It was a baffling moment for them both, because Blamey hadn't meant his words to come across that way, or for his voice to waver when he said them. For a short, awkward moment they stood in silence, and when Lavarack turned to leave, he looked back twice, for along with the triumph on Blamey's face he was sure he saw a trace of sentiment.

"Not long now before he's gone," Blamey was really thinking with glee.

Yet it was the oddest thing ... for when Lavarack's ship set out to sea and sounded its lonely horn, Blamey's throat clenched tight at the thought of how much he'd miss him.

CODA

In the end, it didn't matter whether they liked or loathed each other, when both men, in their different ways, were destined to succeed. The irony was that Blamey, as the consummate politician packaged in military uniform, was to remain in the service and rise to the rank of Australia's first and only Field Marshal. While Lavarack, to whom the uniform meant everything, would finally hang it up for good to become the Governor of Queensland and one of the country's longest-standing statesmen.

EPILOGUE

MAIN CHARACTERS

FM THOMAS BLAMEY

GBE, KCB, CMG, DSO, ED

(24 JANUARY 1884 – 27 MAY 1951)

There was nothing Blamey admired more than a dedicated friend or enemy, but he was never sure which Lavarack was. To cover both contingencies, he continued to sabotage Lavarack's career while never naming the supposed flaws in Lavarack's character that he said made him unsuitable for high command. There was little Lavarack could do to counter the claims, but Blamey's poor treatment of him didn't go unnoticed.

In 1944, Australia's Senator Hattil S. Foll[47] took the floor in parliament to say:

"We don't approve of the way Blamey has shelved Lavarack and other fine officers such as Allen, Potts and Rowell."

Foll was the Minister for Repatriation, and as a former soldier wounded at Gallipoli, he knew the sort of men under whom Australian troops wished to serve.

"When it comes to Lavarack," he continued, "there is scarcely a man in the Australian Army who came through his training with higher honours and a greater reputation after his short, but highly successful command at Tobruk. Yet, because of a personal disagreement with our CIC, that man has been sacrificed and sent halfway round the world to a job he should never have been called upon to take.

Having been put in a bad light, Blamey wrote a letter to his old mate Menzies, who was in political opposition at the time:

> *There was no personal disagreement between General Lavarack and me, nor is there one now. Furthermore, he wasn't removed from active participation in military operations. I'd made sure of that by retaining him in his role as Commander 1st Army located in Australia.*

Menzies wrote a consoling note back:

> *Don't worry about Foll's criticism. As far as I, and many of my colleagues are concerned, you would still be our choice to lead the army.*

Though backing his old friend, Menzies wasn't blind to what Blamey had been doing. Yet, he didn't hold it against him when he knew that sometimes men had to take such cold-blooded measures to stay in power.

The majority of Australians who didn't aspire to as much, however, saw things more clearly and held Blamey accountable throughout the course of his career.

Yet, despite the controversy that continually surrounded him, there was no denying Blamey's commanding presence and the fact that there was something about him that amounted to charm.

–oOo–

"I think I'm dying," he said to the nurse who, in 1951, was attending to him in hospital.

He'd been a difficult patient, but having learnt how to handle him, she scoffed at the idea.

"Nothing can kill you ... you old coot!" she answered with a dismissive click of her fingers."Now sit up and finish your meal."

Her no-nonsense manner did him good, as his using the same had often done for his troops. Where she was concerned, however, the only way he could thank her for all her support was to share with her what to him, at the last, meant the most. Feeling himself fading fast, he said to her with sudden urgency:

"Open my top drawer, over there."

She took from it a box covered in crimson velvet, and on opening it, found his Field Marshal's baton cushioned on blue satin inside. When he saw she was impressed, he only had time to say with a tired, triumphant smile:

"I'm the only Australian to have the honour of owning it."

It was a privilege, that since, hasn't been extended to any other Australian.

–oOo–

Blamey died from a cerebral haemorrhage on May 27, 1951, at the age of 77. Three hundred thousand people lined the streets of Melbourne at his funeral procession, while ten of his lieutenant generals served as pallbearers. One of them, as testimony to the power of forgiveness, was Sydney Rowell.

As the parade passed by to the slow beat of the drum, two of Blamey's best friends – the soon-to-be Sir Robert Menzies and Lord Casey watched on:

"Look Bob, this is astonishing," Casey said in disbelief when he saw tears rolling down so many cheeks.

It was a sight that had Menzies reply with a wry, sad smile:

"Tears for Blamey ... who would have thought?"

LT GEN JOHN LAVARACK
KCMG, KCVO, KBE, CB, DSO
(19 DECEMBER 1885 – 4 DECEMBER 1957)

Lavarack's exile to Washington would last until 1946, with the war going on without him at home for the next 19 months.

Although he went on to serve as the military adviser to the Australian delegation at the United Nations' San Francisco Conference, he never ceased being disappointed by his lack of active command. By the time he returned to Australia, he had been stripped of his fighting spirit.

"Nothing has turned out as I expected," he thought as he winged his way across the Pacific.

His work in Washington had been interesting, but wasn't what he wanted, and while the war had still been on, he'd said as much during an interview with the official historian in the US Capitol.

"Aren't you happy here in Washington?" the American asked him.

To which he answered honestly:

"Everyone in Washington is treating me so well, but it's been a sadly inactive career for me here. I fear that my present activities will not occupy a very large part of your records of this war. Nor my previous ones, for that matter, I imagine. All I want is another battlefield command."

That would never happen while Blamey was in charge, and it was a crime on his part for having hamstrung such a soldier. For Blamey, however, it was a case of self-preservation and of removing the millstone hanging around his neck.

When Lavarack finally surrendered to Blamey's will and put away his uniform for good, he was offered the Governorship of Queensland, and in that capacity served for eleven successful years, seeing the ascent of Queen Elizabeth II to the throne and officially proclaiming her monarch in Queensland.

Although grateful for the opportunities he'd been given, he would forever cast a wistful eye in the direction of what he'd been denied. When he retired due to ill health, he was given a pension of £1000 per annum, but on December 4, 1957, having outlived Blamey by six years, he collapsed from a heart attack at his breakfast table and died.

He was survived by his wife, Sybil and three sons – John, Peter and Wallace, while being honoured with a state funeral. For his service during both world wars, he received a litany of awards[48] and for his outstanding, albeit actively restrained military service, had the Lavarack Barracks in Townsville named after him.

LT GEN SYDNEY ROWELL
KBE, CB
(15 DECEMBER 1894 – 12 APRIL 1975)

Rowell was the Vice Chief of the General Staff from 1946 to 1950, and Chief of the General Staff from 1950 to 1954. Though he played a key role in WWII's reorganisation of the army, he is best known for being the first commander dismissed from the Kokoda Trail Campaign.

That looked bad on his record and the fact that it happened was outrageous. For years to come, it would have serious repercussions throughout the military, and when, three years later, he was restored to the rank of lieutenant general, with the role of CGS – the most senior position in the Australian Army - it was as much to say that those who had formerly accused him were sorry for the shabby way in which he had been treated.

The circumstances of his sacking by Blamey were extraordinary. After it happened, Rowell moved, either from pride or anger, to the War Office in London to take up the appointment of Director of Tactical Investigation, but when Blamey's appointment as Commander-in-Chief terminated in 1945, Australia's new Prime Minister, Ben Chifley, recalled Rowell from Europe to put him in the new post of Vice Chief of the General Staff.

At Chifley's invitation, Rowell went to visit him when he arrived in Canberra.

"I hate bloody injustice!" Chifley told him.

So, for further recompense for having had it inflicted on him, Chifley made sure, in 1950, that Rowell became the first Duntroon graduate to become Chief of the General Staff. It was the beginning of five very successful years, during which Rowell presided over Australia's Korean War expansion of the Regular Army, the National Service Scheme, and the re-establishment of the women's services.

When Rowell retired from the Army after 43 years of military service, he published his memoirs, in which he showed remarkable dignity and restraint in regard to his crisis with Blamey.

It was a fitting way for a man of integrity to leave this world, and in 1975, at the age of eighty, Rowell passed away at his home in South Yarra, Victoria. His death came just twelve days before that of his wife, Blanche, and they left behind them their one daughter, Rosslyn and son-in-law, Professor John Poynter.

There has never been any doubt about Rowell's professional ability, intellectual qualities or strength of character. Yet, the question of whether he failed as a commander in New Guinea, as General Blamey later claimed, or rather was the victim of the coming together of long-term national security weaknesses, has never been determined to the satisfaction of all involved.

MAJ GEN GEORGE ALAN VASEY

CB, CBE, DSO & BAR

(29 MARCH 1895 – 5 MARCH 1945)

The ever-colourful Alan Vasey first found fame during WWI when, as a major, he performed with distinction during the Battles of Messines, Passchendaele, Amiens and the Hindenburg Line.

By the time he reached the rank of lieutenant colonel in WWII, his troops were happily calling him Bloody George,[49] not with disrespect, but because he used the word so frequently and didn't care who called him out on it.

Journalist and military historian, Gavin Long, summed him up:

> *Vasey was highly strung, thrustful and hard-working, but concealed a deeply emotional, even sentimental nature, behind a mask of laconic and blunt speech. Although he was appointed to head the administrative staff, there burned within him a desire to lead Australian troops as a commander.*

In 1942, at the age of 46, he was the youngest general in the Australian Army, having reached the rank of major general.

Yet, despite his achievements, Vasey was twice passed over for promotion. The first time in 1943, when command of II Corps went to his old rival Major General Frank Berryman, rather than him; and then in 1944, when Major General Stanley Savige was given preference to lead I Corps – a decision that rested on Blamey's recommendation for reasons of his own and perhaps in return for a favour.

Even General MacArthur saw Vasey's suppression as being 'outrageous', and was surprised that, though not backing him, Blamey didn't disagree:

"What is really your opinion of Vasey," MacArthur asked him at a social function.[50]

In answer to which, Blamey got to his feet, and pointing to Vasey, called out across the room:

"There, ladies and gentlemen, is my ideal fighting commander."

Blamey, however, was concerned about Vasey's health. He was drinking too heavily and had, in New Guinea and Australia, been hospitalised a few times with respiratory tract infection. When Vasey became seriously ill with malaria, in 1944, he wasn't expected to live.

"Will he?" his loyal troops from the 7th Division kept asking anxiously of the medical staff, for as far as they were concerned, he was the only commanding officer who mattered and they didn't know where they'd be without him.

A Melbourne journalist wrote:

> *Vasey owns the 7th, but every man in the division believes he owns Vasey.*

To their relief, he slowly recovered and, in October, 1944, Blamey set up a Post-War Army Planning Committee headed by Vasey to report on the future of the Royal Military College and the training and education of Staff Corps officers.

Like Lavarack, however, Vasey wasn't happy with administrative work and, in February 1945, Frank Forde, who was serving as Australia's caretaker prime minister for a short seven days after John Curtin's death, pressed for Vasey to be given another active command.

"I still have grave doubts about his physical fitness," Blamey protested, "even though he's been cleared by the Army Medical Board."

Forde, with mounting frustration argued back:

"How often, Blamey, does the man have to prove to you that he's nothing if not resilient?"

With his hand forced, Blamey reluctantly appointed Vasey to command the 6th Division, which in March, 1945, was fighting in New Guinea's Aitape-Wewak Campaign.

–oOo–

"I don't like the look of that brewing storm," the pilot of the RAAF Lockheed Hudson said before taking off from Brisbane's Archerfield Airport to fly Vasey to his new command.

At the centre of that storm was a cyclone that, while ravaging the Queensland's coast, hurled the plane off course, and when its engines cut out and it crashed into the sea, all on board were killed.

Vasey's body was recovered and buried with full military honours in Cairns Cemetery, where Generals Morshead and Blamey were chief mourners – the latter of whom, in all likelihood, felt responsible for having effectively sent him to his death.

EPILOGUE

SUPPORTING CHARACTERS

MAJ GEN ARTHUR 'TUBBY' ALLEN
CB, CBE, DSO, VD
(10 MARCH 1894 – 25 JANUARY 1959)

The nickname "Tubby" was given to Allen, not only in reference to his stocky build, but because of the affection with which he was held by his troops and all Australians.

Having fought and earned the Distinguished Service Order in WWI, he was given command of Australia's 6 Division 16th Brigade at the outbreak of WWII, and as such, led his men in the North African Battles of Bardia and Tobruk, before doing the same during the ill-fated Greek Campaign. In 1941, after switching command to the 7th Division during the invasion of Syria and Lebanon, he was promoted to major general.

Japan's declaration of war saw him recalled to Australia to take charge of operations against the enemy advance along the Kokoda Trail. Although he was successful, he came under what many considered unfair criticism from Generals MacArthur and Blamey for moving too slowly in pursuit of the Japanese across the Owen Stanley Ranges. As a result, he was relieved of command in October 1942.

Allen was an accountant by trade, and after the war became senior partner in the chartered accountancy firm of A. S. Allen & Co., based in Sydney. A profession that seemed so sensible and stable after all he'd seen and done during two world wars, and on retirement, he was happy sticking to the gentler pursuits of playing golf and lawn bowls.

He died of hypertensive cerebrovascular disease at the age of 65 in Concord, leaving behind his wife and two sons. As a man much loved and respected by all, he was given a military funeral, along with the honour of having his portrait hung in the Australian War Memorial Canberra.

LT GEN FRANK BERRYMAN

KCVO, CB, CBE, DSO

(11 APRIL 1894 – 28 MAY 1981)

Often called 'The Forgotten Man', Berryman's name is rarely mentioned and doesn't rank in the annals of famous Australian generals. Yet, of him, Sir John Lavarack would say:

> *Berryman was the best combination of fighting leader, staff officer and administrator in our army. I always thought he'd be hard to beat.*[51]

Unfortunately, Berryman didn't stir the same romantic images as did more vibrant men like Lavarack, Blamey, Rowell and Morshead, but the fact that his name seems only to appear in footnotes greatly belies the importance of his achievements.[52]

He was his own worst enemy for not seeking publicity, but as an intensely private, loyal and assiduous man, he shunned the spotlight, because he was preoccupied with serving his command and army. He was, as one newspaper reporter described him in 1945:

> *A soldier's soldier, cool, ruthless, upright, and without a single trick of showmanship.*

In fact, Berryman thought that those officers who sought notoriety among the press did nothing to help win the war, and were, in his words, not acting "in the best interests of the service."

During WWII, with the rank of full colonel, he was responsible for the staff work for the attacks on both Bardia and Tobruk; while when promoted to brigadier, he became Commander, Royal Artillery, 7th Division, and was in control of 'Berryforce' during the Syria-Lebanon Campaign.

He returned to Australia in 1942 to be made Deputy Chief of the General Staff under Blamey, who then took him to Port Moresby to simultaneously act as Chief of Staff of New Guinea Force. There, Berryman was heavily involved with the planning and execution of both the Salamaua–Lae and Huon Peninsula Campaigns. By November, 1943, he was Acting Commander of II Corps, leading the Battle of Sio.

Through his skill as a staff, liaison and planning officer, Berryman was the man behind the scenes, who made himself indispensable to the army and to commanders like Lavarack, Blamey and MacArthur. It was the dominance of these commanders' personalities, however, that both submerged Berryman's identity and overshadowed the role he played in the defeat of Japan.

Fortunately, with that defeat in August 1945, Berryman's contribution to it was rewarded with an appointment as the official Australian Army representative at the surrender ceremonies in Tokyo Bay. He was immensely proud of that honour and the newspaper called it 'the high point of his career'.

After the war, he hoped to become Chief of the General Staff, but he was seen as a 'Blamey man' by Prime Minister Chifley and his Labor Government colleagues, who disliked the former Commander-in-Chief. As a result, and for other fair-minded reasons, the job, instead, went to Rowell.

Berryman died, aged 87 in 1981 at Rose Bay, Sydney and was cremated with full military honours. At the time of his funeral the Ambassador for Lebanon, Raymond Heneine, wrote in the

Canberra Times:

> *The inhabitants of Jezzine will never forget General Berryman, who liberated their town from the Vichy French. He was, for them, not only a great general, but also a great benefactor who provided food supplies and medical care. In fact, he was the perfect example of humanitarianism.*

BRIGADIER ARTHUR BLACKBURN
VC, CMG, CBE, ED, JP
(25 NOVEMBER 1892 – 24 NOVEMBER 1960)

Prior to WWI, Blackburn was a lawyer and part-time soldier. In 1914, he was assigned to the AIF's 10th Battalion. When it landed at Gallipoli on April 25, 1915, he and another scout were credited with advancing inland faster and further than any other soldier on the day.

He, along with the 10th Battalion then fought on the Western Front at the Battle of Pozieres, where his actions, while leading 50 men, won him the Victoria Cross. He was the first South Australian to earn the award, and he did it at the costliest battle in Australian history.

Come WWII, Blackburn was appointed to the 2nd AIF's 2/3rd Machine Gun Battalion during the Syria–Lebanon Campaign, and as its commander, personally accepted the surrender of Damascus. In early 1942, his battalion, under the name of 'Blackforce,' played a major role in the defence of Java. It was a military move to which Lavarack strongly objected, and he was proved right when Blackburn and his troops were captured by the Japanese and kept prisoners for the rest of the war.

It was under their appalling conditions that Blackburn gained further repute for consistently standing up against the enemy's savage interrogations. Though being repeatedly beaten by them and starved into would-be submission, he refused to give an inch until he finally talked the Japanese into behaving.

It was by sheer determination that he managed to survive, but when he returned to Australia and was met by his family in Melbourne, they were shocked by his skeletal appearance. A man standing nearly 6' tall, who now weighed less than 6 stone.

Blackburn was hospitalised several times during the post-war years, and later died on November 24, 1960, at the age of 67. He was buried with full military honours in the AIF section of Adelaide's West Terrace Cemetery. Many members of the public and hundreds of former members of the 10th and 2/3rd Machine Gun Battalions lined the 3km route from St Peter's Cathedral, while eight brigadiers acted as pallbearers.

His medal set, including his VC, was passed to his son Richard, then to his grandson Tom. It is now on loan to the Australian War Memorial, Canberra, where it is displayed in the Hall of Valour.

GEN HENRY (HARRY) CHAUVEL
GCMG, KCB
(16 APRIL 1865 – 4 MARCH 1945)

Chauvel was a senior officer of the Australian Imperial Force, who fought at Gallipoli and in the Middle East during WWI. He was the first Australian to attain the rank of lieutenant general and later general, while being the first to lead a corps.

As commander of the Desert Mounted Corps, he was responsible for one of the most decisive victories and fastest pursuits in military history at the famous Battle of Beersheba, where in a daring, last-minute cavalry charge by the Australian Light Horse 4th Brigade, he captured the town and its vital wells. It was the last major mounted charge in history that secured a crucial victory in the Sinai and Palestine Campaign.

A feat of astounding fortitude and flair that was immortalised by T.E. Lawrence in his book: *Seven Pillars of Wisdom*.

Chauvel's career would intertwine with both Blamey's and Lavarack's. In Blamey's case, starting with them sailing on the same ship to Egypt at the beginning of WWI and developing into a long-standing working relationship as senior Australian commanders who shaped the Australian Army for decades. While Lavarack served under Chauvel during his long period in office as CGS – a tenure that provided stability and left a legacy and vision for the army which Chauvel passed down to Lavarack as one of his successors. Both being men more farsighted than most, Chauvel and Lavarack perceived the Asia-Pacific as the most logical area for future deployment and continued to shape expeditionary force planning.

Chauvel was one of the most revered of Australians. A man respected by all. During WWII, he was recalled to duty as Inspector in Chief of the Volunteer Defence Corps. Following Brudenell White's death in the Canberra air disaster, it was Chauvel to whom Prime Minister Menzies turned for advice on many military matters.

For his services as commander of the Desert Mounted Corps, Chauvel received awards from Britain, France and Egypt and was mentioned in despatches 11 times. Yet, he remained a simple, straightforward men, who when conferred with vestments and accoutrements of the Order of St Michael and St George by King George V, requested that he be dubbed "Sir Harry" rather than "Sir Henry".

> *He was an outstanding commander, who with calm and courage led from the front. A true "Light Horseman" who never forgot his Australian roots and valued his troops above all else, refusing many an award to ever remain on a level with them.*

PRIME MINISTER JOHN CURTIN

(8 JANUARY 1885 – 5 JULY 1945)

Curtin was Australia's 14th Prime Minister, and from 1941 until his death in 1945, guided the country through WWII. With his skills and character held in high regard by his political contemporaries, he ranked as one of the country's greatest political leaders.

As a young man, he was active in both the Socialist and Labor Parties, and in 1935 stood for election as leader of the latter, which was then in Opposition. Though not expected to win, he did so by one vote, and in October 1941, when the Labor Party was in power, became its leader just two months before Japan's attack on Pearl Harbour.

The fall of Singapore and Darwin being bombed made Curtin realise that the security of Australia no longer rested with Britain, but with the America. To ensure that a firm allegiance between the two countries was confirmed, he placed Australian forces under the command of the American general, Douglas MacArthur with whom he would form a close bond. Curtin's statement published in The Daily Telegraph read:

> *The Australian Government regards the Pacific struggle as primarily one in which the United States and Australia must have the fullest say in its fighting plan. Without any inhibitions of any kind, I make it clear that Australia looks to America, free of any pangs as to our traditional links or kinship with the United Kingdom.*[53]

Curtin knew that Australia would be ignored unless it had a strong voice in Washington, and with that now being MacArthur's, he directed all Australian commanders to treat the American general's orders as if they came from the Australian Government.

Biographer John Edwards wrote:

> *A lesser Australian leader might have grated against MacArthur's vanity, grandiloquent claims and assumption of command, but Curtin did not. He seized the chance to share authority with MacArthur, and refusing to offend his vanity, drew him as close as he could. Of Curtin's military decisions, it was the cleverest, most fruitful, most abidingly successful.*[54]

By the time Curtin was travelling between London and Washington for meetings with Churchill, Roosevelt and other Allied leaders in 1944, he was developing heart disease. With the end of the war in sight, his health suddenly deteriorated dramatically, and at 4:00 am on July 5, 1945, as Australia's 7th Division began its last operation against Japanese forces in the Battle of Balikpapan, he died at the age of 60. His body was laid in state at the King's Hall in Parliament House, and Presbyterian minister, Hector Harrison had this to say in his eulogy:

> *Curtin's Calvary was the anguish of a man of peace who loathed war with all his heart and soul. Yet, by a strange irony of fate, he was chosen by destiny to lead the nation in her hour of direst peril. When the hosts of the North came down like a mighty flood, he did not shrink from the*

hazards of the conflict, but threw himself into his work with an utter devotion which, at length, laid him low and at last called for the supreme sacrifice. We pay him today the homage of a grateful people as one whose name will live forever more in the land he loved.[55]

GEN DOUGLAS MACARTHUR

(26 JANUARY 1880 – 5 APRIL 1964)

As WWII ended, MacArthur was the Supreme Commander for the Allied Powers overseeing the occupation of Japan from 1945 to 1951; and then became Head of the United Nations Command in the Korean War from 1950 to 1951.

During WWII's Pacific War he established a close relationship with Prime Minister John Curtin, and was probably the second-most-powerful person in the nation. Yet many Australians resented a foreign general being imposed upon them, despite the fact that they and their country couldn't have won without him.

Like Blamey, much about MacArthur was controversial. During the Battle of Buna-Gona, he ordered Lieutenant General Robert L. Eichelberger to assume command of the Americans, while moving the advanced echelon of his own GHQ to Port Moresby. When Buna finally fell in January, 1943, MacArthur awarded the Distinguished Service Cross to twelve officers for "precise execution of operations". This use of Australia's second highest award aroused antagonism, because while some, like Generals Eichelberger and Vasey, had fought in the field, other recipients, such as Sutherland and Willoughby, had not.

In other respects, however, MacArthur had foresight and was, in many ways ahead of his time. He championed a progressive approach to the reconstruction of Japan, while contending, in 1941, that Nazi Germany could not defeat the Soviet Union. He argued that North Korea and China were no mere Soviet puppets, throughout his career insisting that the future lay in the Far East. To that end, he implicitly rejected White American contemporary notions of racial superiority and always treated Filipino and Japanese leaders with respect as equals.

With his overbearing vanity and glory-mongering MacArthur will always be the proverbial 'riddle wrapped in a mystery inside an enigma', which made it all the more a wonder that he and Blamey, as a man much the same, managed to work so well together. Neither would ever underestimate the other, while both would clearly see and appreciate each other for what they were. When later asked about MacArthur, Blamey said:

> *The best and the worst things you hear about him are both true.*

While American President Harry S. Truman once remarked:

> *I do not understand how the U.S. Army can produce men such as Robert E. Lee, John J. Pershing, Eisenhower and Bradley, and at the same time produce Custers, Pattons and MacArthur.*

Yet some years later, President John F. Kennedy, before his own death in 1963, set in place instructions that at MacArthur's death (from abdominal surgery in 1964 at the age of 84), he was to be given a state funeral and buried:

> *With all the honor a grateful nation can bestow on a departed hero.*

LT GEN IVEN MACKAY

KBE, CMG, DSO & Bar, VD

(7 APRIL 1882 – 30 SEPTEMBER 1966)

Mackay was nicknamed "Mr Chips", after the famous film *Goodbye Mr. Chips,* not only in reference to his peacetime profession as teacher and Headmaster of Sydney's Cranbrook School, but because of the impression he gave of being cool, reserved and strict. Even his own staff officers had reservations about him, with Colonel Alan Vasey, as his Assistant Adjutant and Quartermaster General, saying that Mackay lacked the ruthlessness to remove officers who weren't performing well, while often fuming about him being:

> *That bloody schoolteacher who wants to dot every 'i' and cross every 't'!*

When Blamey was first elevated to command the Australian Army's newly created 1 Corps, MacKay, on the advice of General Brudenell White, was chosen to command its 7th Division. But with Lavarack set to command the 6th. Blamey did a switch, giving Mackay the 6th, instead, because it was the division due to see action first and he didn't want Lavarack to get the kudos that went with it.

All doubts about Mackay's ability disappeared when, at the Battle of Bardia in 1941, his 6th Division captured the fortified town and took 36,000 Italian prisoners.

His next campaign, at the Battle of Greece, wasn't so successful, with Mackay having to lead a hastily assembled Australian-British-New Zealand-Greek formation, known as 'Mackay Force', at the

Battle of Vevi. He was to be the only Australian general to face the Waffen-SS in battle, and he had to do it against odds that were overwhelming.

As in Libya, Mackay shared the hardships of living in the field with his men, and impressed them by his coolness during air raids. They watched him sit in the open, waiting out a two-and-a-half-hour attack when his car was hit and his driver wounded. One staff officer "noticed Mackay moving in front of his tent quite unconcerned about the enemy planes. He neither looked at them nor at the men dashing about for cover, but when they saw him standing totally unperturbed, those seeking shelter stopped, while the others who'd already found it followed his example and returned to duty."[56]

One lesson of Greece was that modern war was a young man's trade, and in 1941, Mackay handed over command of the 6th to younger General Edmund Herring, while he, himself, with the rank of lieutenant general, took command of Home Forces.

At much the same time that Mackay's son, Iven, became a Japanese prisoner of war, Blamey did a sweeping reorganization and made Mackay Commander of Australia's Second Army. In that role, Mackay assumed command, of New Guinea Force, but that period of command was marred by disagreements with MacArthur's staff over the reinforcement of the port town of Finschhafen. Junior commanders felt that Mackay failed to be forceful enough and that he should have enlisted the help of his superior, General Blamey, at an earlier stage.

Blamey agreed, and feeling that his old colleague no longer possessed the vigour required for the New Guinea Campaign, had him hand over command to Lieutenant General Sir Leslie Morshead, while also relinquishing his command of Second Army.

In recompense, Prime Minister John Curtin, with Blamey's approval, appointed Mackay as High Commissioner to India. A post he filled for the next five years.

Mackay died at his home in East Lindfield, Sydney on September 30, 1966 at the age of 84. Veterans lined the streets during the funeral parade and ten generals acted as his pallbearers. He was survived by his wife, Marjorie, his two daughters, Alison and Ann, and his son, Iven, who had miraculously survived his Japanese imprisonment.

PRIME MINISTER ROBERT MENZIES

(20 DECEMBER 1894 – 15 MAY 1978)

Menzies was twice Prime Minister of Australia: First, as leader of the UAP during 1939 to 1941, and then, in 1949 to 1966 as leader of the relatively new Liberal Party.

He was Australia's longest serving Prime Minister and the first to have two Australian-born parents.

As leader of the country in 1939, he authorised Australia's entry into WWII, declaring Australia's support for Britain in a radio broadcast:

> *Fellow Australians, it is my melancholy duty to inform you, officially, that in consequence of a persistence by Germany in her invasion of Poland, Great Britain has declared war upon her and that, as a result, Australia is also at war.*

He spent four months in Britain discussing war strategy with Churchill and other Empire leaders. It was posited, at this point. that Menzies might have replaced Churchill as British Prime Minister, and that he had some support in the UK for this from Viscount Astor, Lord Beaverbrook and David Lloyd George, who as trenchant critics of Churchill's autocratic style, favoured Menzies as his replacement.

Oh his way to the UK, Menzies had stopped off to visit the Australian troops fighting in North Africa, and Churchill, soon after, asked Menzies to give his approval to send those Australian forces in North Africa to Greece.

Like many other Australians of his generation, Menzies was haunted by the memory of Gallipoli, which had come about due to Churchill sending an Allied force to the Dardanelles, and he was highly suspicious of another of Churchill's plans for victory in the Mediterranean. However, on February 25, 1941, Menzies reluctantly gave his approval to send Australia's 6th Division to Greece.

His reputation suffered badly as a result, and an article in an Australian newspaper read:

> *Menzies too readily acquiesced in the ill-starred Greek Campaign. As a military adventure it was madness. As a political gesture, it was even more stupid, because it was doomed to failure.*

To ease the burden of criticism, Menzies passed the buck to Blamey, maintaining that he'd only given his permission to send the Australian troops to Greece because Blamey hadn't opposed the idea:

> *If Blamey had shown his disapproval as a professional soldier, I would never have sent our Australians to Greece.*

Matters came to a head when it was voted to have Menzies return to London to speak for Australia's interests in the War Cabinet. However, now that both Australian political parties were on par, Menzies needed the Labor Party's consent to go. With the world in crisis, and rumours of Menzies' real intention being to launch a political career in Britain, Labor refused to let him to leave the country.

Labor took government in October 1941 and though Menzies fell back to lead the Opposition, he was to become Prime Minister again in 1949, during which time he was back on Blamey's side and was resolved to have made a Field Marshal. It was a suggestion that didn't go down well in Britain.

"A dominion officer cannot be promoted to that rank," the King's Official Secretary, Sir Alan Lascelles said.

"That can't be true," Menzies argued. "Considering that South Africa's General Jan Smuts has recently been extended the honour."

That, Lascelles couldn't deny, so he fought on, saying instead: "Besides, Blamey can't be promoted to Field Marshal because he's a retired officer."

"Well, I can fix that!" Menzies said, moving immediately to restore Blamey to active duty, despite the man being gravely ill in hospital.

For Menzies, it was a matter of principle after all Blamey had done for his country, and Menzies, himself, presented the Field Marshal's baton standing at his old friend's bedside in 1950.

Twenty-eight years later, Menzies, died from a heart attack at the age of 84. Tributes rolled in from around the world, notably from Elizabeth II, Queen of Australia:

> *I was distressed to hear of the death of Sir Robert Menzies. He was a distinguished Australian whose contribution to his country and the Commonwealth will long be remembered.*

The country's own Prime Minister Malcolm Fraser said more:

> *All Australians will mourn his passing. Sir Robert leaves an enduring mark on Australian history.*

GEN JOHN MONASH
GCMG, KCB, VD
(27 JUNE 1865 – 8 OCTOBER 1931)

Monash was a civil engineer who, in 1887, joined the university company of the militia. By 1908, he had been promoted to lieutenant colonel in the intelligence corps, and at the outbreak of WWI, was given command of the 4th Brigade with which he fought at Gallipoli.

He and his Brigade defended the line between Pope's Hill and Courtney's Post and the valley behind that line was named after him. Although, due to his German-Jewish ancestry, rumours abounded about him being a "German Spy", he was promoted to brigadier general and in 1916 was transferred to the Western Front where, as a major general, he took command of the Australian 3rd Division.

He led that division through the Battles of Messines, Broodseinde and the First Battle of Passchendaele, with British Field Marshal Haig being so impressed by him that he wanted Monash as a corps commander. By June 1918, Monash was a lieutenant general in command of the Australian Corps – the largest individual corps, at the time, on the Western Front.

The Battle of Hamel, in 1918, saw Monash, with the help of the British and a detachment of American troops, win a significant victory. After which, with 208,000 men under his command, he planned and broke through the Hindenburg Line. A success that had the German Government ask for an immediate armistice.

By war's end, Monash had acquired an outstanding reputation for intellect, personal magnetism, management and ingenuity. He had also won the respect and loyalty of his troops with his motto:

Feed your troops on victory.

The British held him in high regard, with a captain from the 8th Division describing him as:

> *A great bullock of a man; though his manners are pleasant and his behaviour far from rough, I have seen few men who gave me such a sensation of force. A fit leader for the wild men he commanded.*

But it was Field Marshal Bernard Montgomery who summed him up best:

> *I would name Sir John Monash as the best general on the Western Front.*

Monash's impact on the Australian military was three-fold. He was the first Australian to fully command Australian forces, and as such, took an independent line with his British superiors. He promoted the concept of the commander's duty to ensure the safety and well-being of his troops. And finally, he, along with his staff officer, Thomas Blamey, forcefully demonstrated the benefit of thorough planning and integration of all arms of the forces available, and of all the components supporting the front line forces, including logistical, medical and recreational services.

Troops later recounted that one of the most extraordinary things about the Battle of Hamel was not the use of armoured tanks, nor the tremendous success of the operation, but the fact that, in the midst of battle, Monash arranged delivery of hot meals up to the front line.

LT GEN LESLIE MORSHEAD
KCB, KBE, CMG, DSO, ED
(18 SEPTEMBER 1889 – 26 SEPTEMBER 1959)

Morshead was a teacher, businessman and farmer, with a military career that would span both world wars. During the Second, he led the Australian and British troops at the Siege of Tobruk and at the Second Battle of El Alamein, where he achieved decisive victories over Erwin Rommel's *Afrika Korps.* With Morshead's habit of squinting and stroking his chin when deep in thought, his troops nicknamed him "Ming the Merciless", later simply "Ming" after the villain in the Flash Gordon comics.

At the onset of WWI, he, with the 2nd Infantry Battalion, landed at Anzac Cove and advanced further than any other Australian unit on the day. Later wounded and suffering from dysentery, he was invalided to Australia, but as soon as he recovered, he became commander of the 33rd Infantry Battalion, which he led on the Western Front at the Battles of Messines, Passchendaele, Viller-Bretonneux and Amiens.

He was promoted to major and distinguished himself at the Battle of Lone Pine, where the fighting was so intense that of the 22 officers in the battalion, Morshead was the only one who did not become a casualty. For his outstanding work he was awarded the Distinguished Service Order, with his citation written by his Division Commander, Major General John Monash.

Official historian, Charles Bean, described Morshead as:

> *A dapper little schoolmaster, only 28 years of age, in whom the traditions of the British Army had been bottled from his childhood like tight-corked*

champagne. Yet, he had turned out a battalion which was recognised as one of the very best.

During WWII, he was in command of the Australian 9th Division at the Siege of Tobruk, where their famously tenacious defence of the North African port earned them the nickname: "Rats of Tobruk". Morshead was a key figure in the prolonged defence of the port, bettering his orders by holding it for five months rather than the required eight weeks. In having done so, he established himself as one of the most respected and toughest leaders in the Australian Army.

Morshead summed himself up in his attitude towards the British propaganda article entitled:

Tobruk can take it!

He responded:

We're not here to take it. We're here to give it!

At the Second Battle of El Alamein, his 9th Division was tasked with clearing a corridor through the enemy forces in the North. When the British attack faltered, the main effort switched to his Australians, who punched a massive dent into the enemy's position, 'crumbling" the Afrika Korps, and in the process, forcing Rommel to retreat.

In high praise, British Lieutenant General Oliver Leese said to Morshead:

I am quite certain that this breakout was made possible by Homeric fighting over your divisional sector.

However, it came at a huge cost: 1,177 Australians were dead, 3,629 wounded, and while 795 were captured, 193 men had gone missing.

According to Official historian Barton Maughan:

> *Morshead was every inch a general. His slight build and seemingly mild facial expression masked a strong personality, the impact of which, even on a slight acquaintance, was quickly felt.*

Montgomery would later add to that:

> *Where there were contests of wills, Morshead was not likely to be found wanting.*

In November, 1943, Morshead became acting commander of New Guinea Force and Second Army. Blamey placed Vasey's 7th Division directly under Morshead's command, but Vasey soon chafed under it feeling that:

> *Morshead has too many favourites, with the men who served at El Alamein receiving preferential treatment.*

Nonetheless, Morshead remained in overall charge of the forces in New Guinea during the Battles of Sattelberg, Jivevaneng, Sio and Shaggy Ridge. His perseverance was rewarded with the capture of Madang in April 1944.

When he handed over command to Lieutenant General

Stanley Savige in May, 1944, many claimed that he'd been 'shelved'. Yet Blamey, in fact, had recommended to Curtin that Morshead should succeed him as commander-in-chief in the event that he became incapacitated.

Although Morshead was pleased at the recognition, he'd never liked dealing with politicians and he felt himself fortunate that it never happened.

Morshead died of cancer in September 1959 at St Vincent's Hospital, Sydney. He was given a military funeral at which former soldiers of the 9th Division paid their respects. He was survived by his wife, Myrtle and daughter, Elizabeth.

SIR KEITH MURDOCH

(12 AUGUST 1885 – 4 OCTOBER 1952)

Murdoch was an Australian journalist and media proprietor who founded the Murdoch media empire. He amassed significant media holdings in Australia which, after his death, were expanded globally by his son, Rupert.

He was a war correspondent during World War I. and his attacks on the Allied high command's conduct in the Gallipoli campaign brought him to the attention of senior British politicians and press barons, including Lord Northcliffe and Australian Prime Ministers Andrew Fisher and Billy Hughes.

Contemptuous of the Gallipoli Campaign's mismanagement, he wrote a letter to Fisher criticising the British administrative staff and General Ian Hamilton, who was in overall command there:

> *The conceit and self complacency of the red-feather men are equaled only by their incapacity. Along the line of communications are countless high officers and vain young cubs, who are plainly only playing at war. Most of them, not having a clue what they're doing, but being appointed to the general staff from motives of friendship and social influence.*[57]
>
> —*Murdoch*

His letter soon gained the attention of British Prime Minister Herbert Asquith, and it was primarily responsible for Hamilton being relieved of command and Gallipoli being evacuated as fast as possible.

Murdoch's opinion was beginning to matter. In 1931, he backed Joseph Lyons to become Prime Minister, but later regretting it said with alarming confidence:

I put him there and I'll put him out!

By 1935, as editor of The Herald in Melbourne, Murdoch had co-founded The Australian Associated Press (AAP) and was the inaugural Chairman of Australian Newsprint Mills. With his voice now strong in matters political, civil and military, there was genuine concern about the power of the press being in the hands of one man. This came to a head when, in WWII, Murdoch was made Director-General of Information, in which role he obtained authorisation to compel all news media to publish Government statements as and when necessary. Comparisons were made with Goebbels, and with all politicians protesting, Murdoch was obliged to resign the position.

He spent the rest of the war encouraging a patriotic spirit, while forever at loggerheads with Blamey and Labor Prime Minister, John Curtin.

Murdoch died of cancer at the age of 67 in October 1952. Much of his estate was disposed of in paying mortgages and death duties, but his family was still left with full control of News Limited. By any standards, he was a remarkable man.

BRIGADIER ARNOLD POTTS

DSO, OBE, MC

(16 SEPTEMBER 1896 – 1 JANUARY 1968)

Potts served in WWI, and later, in WWII, commanded the 21st Brigade against the Japanese during the Kokoda Trail Campaign.

His leadership and the brigade's fighting withdrawal has been described as:

> *One of the most critical triumphs in Australian military history, and one that an apathetic nation has still to honour.*[58]

While the Battle of Brigade Hill for Potts and his 21st Brigade was a tactical defeat, their efforts in this and earlier battles along the Kokoda Trail were a critical part of the overall strategy. One which delayed the Japanese advance and strained their supply lines to breaking point.

Unfortunately for Potts, the Japanese, with the help of local guides, found their way through the jungle terrain, and cutting off his 21st Brigade's 2/14, 2/16 and 2/27 battalions, forced them into a scattered retreat. The men of those battalions were already under-strength, and with them suffering from disease, exhaustion, and the lack of food and ammunition, it was difficult for them to keep up a sustained defence. It took the 2/27 weeks to rejoin their main force due to their torturous jungle march carrying their stretcher-bound dead and wounded.

Under appalling conditions, theirs was a story of stamina and supreme courage, yet despite his 21st having helped halt the Japanese advance, Potts had to endure its men being called cowards, while he, himself, was relieved of command by Blamey in October 1942. A decision that has since sparked much debate, considering that most of Potts' contemporaries saw his dismissal as being unfair and believed it to be one of the most controversial decisions of Blamey's career.

Some historians believe that Potts was a scapegoat removed by Blamey to avoid a showdown with MacArthur, who had told the Chief of Staff of the United States Army that:

> *The Australians have proven themselves unable to match the enemy in jungle fighting and aggressive leadership is lacking.*

In response, it was suggested that Blamey's removal of Potts was simply a case of self-preservation.

Following the war, Potts returned to farming in Western Australia and briefly, albeit unsuccessfully, attempted to pursue a career in politics. In the 1960s, he became reliant on a wheelchair after a series of strokes, and died at the age of 71 in January, 1968.

LT GEN STANLEY SAVIGE
KBE, CB, DSO, MC, ED
(26 JUNE 1890 – 15 MAY 1954)

Savige served in both World Wars and was twice recommended for the Military Cross for bravery: Once, for his actions at the Battle of Bullecourt, and then again at Passchendaele.

During the early years of WWII, Blamey selected Savige to command his 6th Division's 17th Infantry Brigade, because they had always worked well together and Savige was almost fanatically loyal to Blamey through good times and bad. Something Savige had proved by backing up Blamey's alibi during his troublesome Police Commissioner days.

Savige's 17th Brigade fought at the Battles of Bardia and Tobruk, and then at the Battle of Greece, before taking part in the Syria–Lebanon Campaign. In most instances, the 17th played a vital role in delaying the German advance so that thousands of their fellow Allied troops could evacuate.

When Savige returned to Australia in early 1942, he was given command of the 3rd Division during the Salamaua–Lae Campaign, and when promoted to lieutenant general, commanded the Australian II Corps in the Bougainville Campaign.

Blamey, however, had serious concerns about Savige's capacity when his 3rd Division was first alerted to move to New Guinea in February 1943:

"It's tough going up there, and I have doubts about Savige's physical fitness," he said.

But a thorough medical examination cleared the way and Savige set off for Port Moresby.

His mandate was to threaten the Japanese position at Salamaua, and despite the rugged conditions, Savige worked hard at proving Blamey wrong by leading from the front, visiting forward positions and flying over frontline areas sporting his scarlet general's cap band to let his men and Japanese snipers know that the general was on the job.

In February 1944, there was a vacancy as head of I Corps, and while Vasey and Savige were nominated for the role, Blamey's recommendation rested with the latter. When Army Minster, Frank Forde queried this, Blamey assured him that Savige was the better man for the job, but General MacArthur considered Vasey's supersession "Outrageous!"

Bougainville, in April 1944, was to be Savige's sixth and last campaign. With him leading 1 Corps, (now re-designated as II), it was to be the only one free of controversy about his command. For it cost a relatively small 516 Australian lives, compared to 8,500 Japanese being killed in action and another 9,800 dying of other causes. By the end of the war, just 23,571 Japanese troops were left alive, and on September 8, 1945, Savige accepted their surrender at Torokina.

SIR FREDERICK SHEDDEN

(8 AUGUST 1893 - 8 JULY 1971)

Shedden was a public servant born in Victoria. He began work in the Department of Defence at Victoria Barracks in 1910, and apart from service overseas, was to work there until 1971.

He attended the London Imperial Defence College with fellow student, Brevet Colonel Lavarack in 1927, and was the first Australian civilian to do so with what his mentor, Vice-Admiral Sir Herbert Richmond described as 'acuteness and zeal'. He and Lavarack, however, were rarely of one mind, and it was to remain that way for the rest of their careers.

When Shedden returned to Melbourne in 1929, looking very short and trim in his pinstripe suit, he was appointed Secretary of the Defence Committee and took part in debates between senior naval and army officers over the most appropriate strategy for defending Australia. He was ever pro-England and in an effort to support its Royal Navy, his argument to build up the Australian Navy in preference to its Army clashed with Lavarack's most strongly held views.

In 1932, he was also appointed Australian representative to the British Cabinet Office, and to the Committee of Imperial Defence at which he established a friendship with the influential Sir Maurice (Baron) Hankey. The man of the day in whose shadow Shedden followed so closely that the British press took to calling him: "The Pocket Hankey".

A label Shedden didn't mind when, in 1937, it lead to him becoming Secretary of the Australian Department of Defence.

As such, Shedden was an aloof and distant figure who 'eschewed publicity'. His whole life revolved around his work and he spent most of his time at the office, while he and his wife lived modestly without children.

He was a man ever conscious of his status, and while some military chiefs such as Major General Lavarack and Air Vice-Marshal Richard Williams resented his power, Admiral Sir Ragnar Colvin, Commander of the Australian Royal Navy at the outbreak of WWII said:

> *Shedden always had the ear of the Prime Minister and could generally get the Chiefs of Staff's view and wishes overridden. Still, he was an able and knowledgeable man and though one couldn't trust him personally, his views were generally sound.*

The outbreak of World War II made Shedden Australia's most important public servant. He was the head of the Department of Defence, but the prime source of his power and influence was his position as Secretary of the War Cabinet, a post he held throughout the war.

In 1940, he also became Secretary of the Advisory War Council and accompanied Menzies on his visit to troops in the Middle East. There to discuss military matters with Blamey, before travelling on to Britain in the hope of persuading its government to reinforce Malaya and Singapore. It was in London that Menzies approved the fatal decision to send forces to Greece.

When the Labor party came to office in October 1941, Shedden soon established himself as principal adviser to Prime Minister John Curtin. Such was Curtin's faith in him that when General Douglas MacArthur became Commander-in-Chief of the South-West Pacific Area, Curtin informed him:

If I should not be readily available, Mr Shedden has my full confidence in regard to all questions of War Policy.

Curtin would later say to Shedden himself:

Without your assistance, I could not have carried on. You are my right and left hand and head too.

Shedden served successfully under a series of prime ministers but finally, by the end of Menzies' second run in the role, he began to wane.

When he died at the age of 77 in July 1971, Sir Frederick Chilton, as one of his subordinates, had this to say:

Shedden had a real presence and powerful personality. He was ruthless with those who crossed him, and devastating with those in his department who could not rise to his exceptional standards of performance. He ruled by fear – and this stultified initiative. But as a head of a small policy Department of Defence, he was superb.

LT GEN VERNON STURDEE

KBE, CB, DSO

(16 APRIL 1890 – 25 MAY 1966)

As a regular officer of the Royal Australian Engineers who joined the Militia in 1908, Sturdee was one of the original Anzacs during WWI. He participated at Gallipoli and commanded the 8th Field Company and 4th Pioneer Battalion on the Western Front.

During WWII, he would work closely with Blamey, Lavarack and Rowell as senior army officers:

He and Blamey had a long and significant professional relationship, serving together as the two most senior Australian Army officers during WWII, with Sturdee acting under Blamey in senior roles.

Sturdee was Head of the Australian Military Mission to Washington D.C in 1942, and consistent with Blamey's promise to return him to an operational command when he came home to Australia, he was put in command of First Australian Army in 1944, in which role he directed significant operations against the Japanese in New Guinea, New Britain, and Bougainville.

When the war ended, Sturdee took the surrender of Japanese forces in the Rabaul area, and in December 1945, following public and political pressure leading to Blamey's removal, Sturdee succeeded him as the Commander-in-Chief of the Australian Military Forces. Four months later, the C-in-C position was closed, and Sturdee resumed the duties of Chief of the General Staff – a position he had previously held in 1940-1942.

While some officers were critical of Blamey, there was a level of mutual respect between the two men. They attended dinners and functions together, and Sturdee was one of the pallbearers at Blamey's funeral in 1951.

Sturdee's connection with Lavarack was almost as strong. He succeeded Lavarack as Director of Military Operations and Intelligence and would later command troops involved in the Java campaign, where Lavarack was also present, leading to their professional interaction and differing opinions on strategy.

Yet both shared a strategic perspective in expressing their doubts about the effectiveness of the "Singapore strategy" and the feasibility of using Australian forces to advantage in Java. Theirs was a deep involvement in that defense of the Dutch East Indies, with Lavarack in overall command of the Australian troops sent to the Java region, while Sturdee, as Chief of the General Staff, sent the urgent order for Lavarack's staff to evacuate as the situation deteriorated.

In essence, they shared strategic concerns and interacted directly during a crucial phase of the Pacific War, with Sturdee often in a superior command role to Lavarack by 1942.

Sturdee and Rowell, too, had a crucial professional partnership, beginning in the 1930s, where they were close colleagues, and culminating post-WWII, with Sturdee appointing Rowell as Vice Chief of the General Staff. Rowell would later succeed Sturdee as Chief of the General Staff, and they would work together to shape Australia's post-war Army.

They shared mutual respect, with Rowell viewing Sturdee as a mentor and reliable leader, and Sturdee recognising Rowell's ability, forming a bedrock for modernising the Australian Army, shaping its structure and response to the emerging Cold War challenges.

Sturdee died on 25 May 1966, and accorded a funeral with full military honours, was cremated, with his boyhood friend, Lieutenant General Sir Edmund Herring, acting as principal pallbearer. He was survived by his wife, their daughter and one of their two sons. Before he died, he burned all his private papers and said:

"I have done the job. It is over."

FM ARCHIBALD WAVELL

GCB, GCSI, GCIE, CMG, MC, PC

(5 MAY 1883 – 24 MAY 1950)

Wavell, as a senior officer of the British Army, served in the Boer and First World War. During WWII, he was initially Commander-in-Chief Middle East, and then of India from 1941 to 1943. For a month in 1942, he also did a stint as Supreme Commander of the South West Pacific American-British-Dutch-Australian Command.

He and Blamey clashed over strategy and control of Australian troops in Greece and Tobruk, with friction between them mounting when Wavell approached Australian Prime Minister Menzies to suggest sending Australian troops to Greece without consulting Blamey. As a result, Blamey fiercely advocated for his AIF's welfare against British high command decisions, ultimately forcing Wavell's and Churchill's hand on the issue.

The professional relationship between Wavell and Lieutenant General Lavarack was also marked by significant command tensions and disagreements over strategy, particularly during the 1941 Syria-Lebanon Campaign.

The primary source of conflict was that Wavell, with his priorities lying elsewhere, severely underestimated the Vichy French resistance and the difficulty of the rugged terrain. As Commander of Australia's 7th Division, and the majority of the campaign, Lavarack argued that Wavell, as his British superior, "had not the least comprehension of the differences between the Lebanon and the African desert". While Wavell expected a victory in Syria within one or two days, Lavarack knew it was totally unrealistic.

They crossed swords again after the Japanese invasion of Malaya. Wavell wanted the returning Australian I Corps, at this point under Lavarack's command, to go to Burma to stem the Japanese tide, but Lavarack and the Australian Government insisted that they return to protect Australia, correctly assessing that Java, as another of Wavell's proposed destinations, was already a lost cause.

On this, Lavarack and the Australian Government stood firm, and the troops eventually came home, despite the 2/2 and 2/4 Pioneer Battalions of their ill-fated Blackforce, having already been sent to Batavia in defense of Java. There, to follow Wavell's senseless order and to suffer the dire consequences of Japanese imprisonment.

The relationship between Wavell and Lavarack, throughout, was strained, primarily due to differing perspectives on local conditions, the allocation of scarce resources, and the overall strategic priorities of the British versus Australian high commands during critical periods of the war.

FM HENRY 'JUMBO' WILSON

GCB, GBE, DSO

(5 SEPTEMBER 1881 – 31 DECEMBER 1964)

Wilson was Commander of the Commonwealth Expeditionary Force in Greece, and was generally thought to be a competent commander, but one historian called him: "a remarkable monument to mediocrity".

He and Blamey, who lead the Anzac Corps, had significant professional interactions, most notably during that ill-fated Greek campaign. Their biggest point of contention occurred when Wilson ordered Blamey to detach an Australian brigade from his force during operations in the Middle East. Blamey refused the order, standing firm in his commitment to keep his troops under Australian command. Prime Minister Winston Churchill eventually backed down, which was a testament to Blamey's resolve for Australian independence in military matters.

Yet, historian Dr Peter Ewer criticised both commanders for their performance at that point in the war, calling Wilson a mediocre leader and Blamey an ineffective commander, who also took an opportunity to leave Greece and his beleaguered Anzac Corps prematurely.

Lavarack, too, worked with Wilson, when the latter was in overall control of the Allied troops in the Middle East and Syria, and Lavarack, who commanded the 7th Division, took control of the Australian 1 Corps. As such, they clashed regularly over the nature of the campaign and the enemy they faced.

Much of the problem was that Wilson was running the operation from his headquarters in Jerusalem, which was 160km from the front lines. Commands coming from such a great distance caused a series of initial setbacks. The most dangerous of which, Lavarack believed, was that both Generals Wilson and Wavell severely underestimated the capacity of the Vichy French and the difficulty of the terrain.

Lavarack wrote in a private letter:

> *Both Wilson and Wavell are hoping that the Vichy French won't even put up a token resistance.*

The Vichy French, however, made such a savage show of it that the Allied forces became bogged down in their initial attacks. It was fortunate, at this point, that Lavarack had been given command of the Australian 1 Corps, for with his new rank of lieutenant general, he assumed overall command of the ground operations for the rest of the campaign. Soon after, his Australian troops captured the pivotal town of Damour, and when they turned, in their strength, to take Beirut, the Vichy French commander, General Henri Dentz, sought an armistice on July 14, 1941.

GEN BRUDENELL WHITE
KCB, KCMG, KCVO, DSO
(23 SEPTEMBER 1876 – 13 AUGUST 1940)

Bar General John Monash, no soldier was more highly regarded than General Brudenell White during WWI. He was instrumental in the creation and operation of the Australian Imperial Force and was considered to be its tactical and administrative commander in all but name.

As Brigadier General, General Staff for the Anzac Corps, he was the mastermind behind the successful, 'silent' evacuation of Gallipoli's Anzac Cove in December 1915. His meticulous planning and tactics ensured the withdrawal of over 80,000 men without a single casualty. A phenomenal success in the otherwise failed campaign.

White's central challenge was to withdraw the large Australian force from Anzac Cove without alerting the enemy, and based on a plan of elaborate deception, he began by implementing short periods of 'silent stunts', during which all artillery fire and sniping from his Allied lines ceased, leading the Turks to think that the Australians were quietly making winter preparations. Irregular firing from the Australian lines would then resume, reinforcing the illusion of normal activity, while in fact, his troops and their equipment, were slowly being withdrawn from the beach.

Then followed his innovative 'Drip Rifle' ruse, with devices rigged to his men's unmanned rifles, that slowly dripped water until the build-up of its weight pulled the trigger, providing sporadic fire from the abandoned trenches long after the last man had left the front line.

The Australian sick and wounded were moved out first, along with their equipment, while under the cover of darkness, the rest of the troops were evacuated bit by bit. By the night of December 19-20, the last 10,000 Australian troops had left Gallipoli's shores.

Monash described it as:

A wonderful piece of organisation.

There wasn't a time when White didn't have the respect of his superiors, peers and subordinates. Until the day he died, he was held in the highest esteem.

Official War Correspondent Charles Bean described him as:

The greatest man he ever knew.

While Monash called him:

Far and away the ablest soldier Australia has ever turned out.

But no one esteemed him more than Blamey, who as a young intelligence officer worked with him extensively during The Great War. The feeling was mutual and at the outbreak of WWII, when White was recalled from retirement to become the Australian Chief of the General Staff, his first action was to recommend Lieutenant General Blamey to command the newly formed Second AIF.

Together, they planned to, once again, work wonders, but sadly, Blamey was destined to run the show alone, for on August 13, 1940, only four months into White's tenure, he was tragically killed when the RAAF Lockheed Hudson Bomber on which he was flying from Melbourne, crashed on its approach to Canberra.

When it mattered most Australia had lost the man it needed at the helm, but Blamey had benefitted from all that White had taught him, and striving to live up to his standards, would forever call him:

The maker of the AIF.

AUTHOR'S NOTE

This is a work of fact-based fiction.
For history's sake it has been kept close to the truth,
but fictionalised conversation and slight shifts in
time sequence have sometimes been used
to link the characters and events.

BIBLIOGRAPHY

BLAME ME

BLAMEY: CONTROVERSIAL SOLDIER
By John Hetherington
The Australian War Memorial and
The Australian Government Publishing Service
CANBERRA, AUSTRALIA 1973

....

FAITHFUL IN ADVERSITY
THE ROYAL ARMY MEDICAL CORPS IN
THE SECOND WORLD WAR
By John Broom
Pen & Sword Military
YORKSHIRE, UK 2019
Imprint of Pen & Sword Books Ltd
PHILADELPHIA, USA

....

FORGOTTEN ANZACS
CAMPAIGN IN GREECE
By Peter Ewer
Scribe Publications 2008
BRUNSWICK, VICTORIA, AUSTRALIA 2008

....

GREECE
FEBRUARY – APRIL 1941
By Michael Tyquin
Big Sky Publishing
SYDNEY, AUSTRALIA 2014

....

LAVARACK: RIVAL GENERAL
By Brett Lodge
Robinson Reynolds,
LONDON, UK 2021

....

THE OFFICIAL HISTORY OF AUSTRALIA IN THE WAR OF 1914-1918 Vol.1
By CEW Bean
SYDNEY, AUSTRALIA 1920

....

ONLINE

THE ANZAC PORTAL
Landing at Anzac Cove 25 April 1915
anzacportal.dva.gov.au

....

AUSTRALIAN DICTIONARY OF BIOGRAPHY
Sir Thomas Albert Blamey
adb.anu.edu.au

....

THE 2/11 AUSTRALIAN INFANTRY BATTALION
awm.gov.au

....

THE COMMANDERS
AUSTRALIAN MILITARY LEADERSHIP
IN THE TWENTIETH CENTURY
Edited by D.M Horner
Allen & Unwin Sydney Australia 1984
National Library of Australia
Routledge Library Edition:
Historical Security.

Specifically:

Lieutenant-General Sir Sydney Rowell:
Dismissal of a Corps Commander
By D.M. Horner

Field Marshal Sir Thomas Blamey:
Commander-in-Chief, Australian Military Forces
By D.M. Horner

Lieutenant-General Sir John Lavarack:
From Chief of the General Staff to Corps Commander
By A.B. Lodge

....

THE FORGOTTEN MAN:
LIEUTENANT GENERAL SIR FRANK BERRYMAN
awm.gov.au

....

BATTLE OF BRALLOS PASS:
ANZACS HOLD THE LINE
History Guild
historyguild.org

....

HOW CHURCHILL LED BRITAIN TO VICTORY
IN THE SECOND WORLD WAR
By James Taylor
iwm.org.uk/history

....

REMEMBERING THE ANZACS AT VEVI
Neos Kosmos
neoskosmos.com

....

THE 'STUNNED' AND THE 'STYMIED': THE POW EXPERIENCE IN THE HISTORY OF THE 2/11 INFANTRY BATTALION, 1939-1945
By Mary R. Watt
Edith Cowan University
Theses: Doctorates and Masters
Research online:
ro.ecu.edu.au
....

WIKIPEDIA

Major General Arthur Samuel 'Tubby' Allen
en.wikipedia.org/wiki/Arthur_Allen

Lieutenant General Sir Frank Horton Berryman
en.wikipedia.org/wiki/Frank_Berryman

Field Marshal, Sir Thomas Albert Blamey
en.wikipedia.org/wiki/Thomas_Blamey

Sir Winston Leonard Spencer Churchill
en.wikipedia.org/wiki/Winston_Churchill

John Curtin
en.wikipedia.org/wiki/John_Curtin

Lieutenant General Sir John Dudley Lavarack
en.wikipedia.org/wiki/John_Lavarack

Lieutenant General Sir Sydney Fairbairn Rowell
en.wikipedia.org/wiki/Sydney_Rowell

Major General George Alan Vasey
en.wikipedia.org/wiki/George_Alan_Vasey

Field Marshal Archibald Percival Wavell
en.wikipedia.org/wiki/Archibald_Wavell

Field Marshal Henry Maitland Wilson, 1st Baron Wilson
en.wikipedia.org/wiki/Henry_Maitland_Wilson

....

ENDNOTES

1. Private Arthur Blackburn and Lance Corporal Philip Robin of the 10th Battalion were the first ashore at Gallipoli at around 4.30am. They penetrated further inland than any other Australians at Anzac Cove. Robin was killed later on 25 April, but Blackburn soldiered on to be commissioned as an officer and awarded the Victoria Cross at Pozieres, the battalion's first major battle in France.
2. Lieutenant Talbot Smith was in charge of the 10th Battalion scouts. Commanding Officer of the10th Battalion Lieutenant Colonel Stanley Price wrote to Smith's parents to say that all Smith's men had been killed or wounded, yet he continued to man the machine guns until he received a head wound. Red Cross relief arrived, but because they thought he was dead, he was not removed for some hours. When he was found to be living he was transported to a hospital ship, and was believed to have died and been buried at sea. He actually lived to reach Alexandria, but died in the hospital there. He was mentioned in despatches for conspicuous gallantry.
3. Lieutenant Colonel Mustafa Kemal said this to his men before leading their attack at the Battle of Sari Bair as part of the Gallipoli August,1915 Offensive.
4. Paraphrase of Gallipoli historian, Robin Prior.
5. Plateau 400 was south-east of Anzac Cove. It was the site of the Battle of Lone Pine, August 6-10,1915.
6. Paraphrase of war correspondent, Charles Bean citing the words of Major General Bridges.
7. Quotation by official War Correspondent C.E.W. Bean.
8. Paraphrase of letters between the Raws brothers on the Villers-Bretonneux. One brother wrote to another, believing that

brother to still be alive. He wasn't and the author of note would die soon after sending it: (Source Alec and Goldthorpe Raws letters from the Western Front awm.com.au). It is estimated that the their 23rd Battalion lost an estimated 90 percent of its original members in the fighting around Pozières in July and August 1916. Both men were lieutenants.

9. Charles Bean
10. Paraphrase on of Monash's acknowledgement of Blamey's role in the Australian Corps' success in the Battle of Amiens and the Battle of the Hindenburg Line.
11. Paraphrase of Sir Maurice Hankey's formal 1934 Report.
12. Paraphrase of Major General Lavarack's report.
13. Paraphrase of Australia's Minister of Defence, Sir Archdale Parkhill's response to Lavarack's assessment of Hankey's report.
14. Britain's Naval Secretary in 1937 was Rear-Admiral William Jock Whitworth. These were not his thoughts or words.
15. This quotation actually came from Billy Hughes who was the former prime minister and at this point being the minister for external affairs, was one of the few ministers who concurred with Lavarack.
16. Paraphrase of Brendan Spencer: Historyguild.org
17. Captain Wilson "Bill" Stewart, Australian Signal Corps was a Militia officer prior to the Second World War and when he enlisted in the Second AIF he was issued the regimental number NX96. He sailed on the troopship "Otranto" in 1939 for the Middle East with 16 Brigade of 6 Division. He was a Lieutenant when he stepped on the ship and a Captain by the time he disembarked. He was killed on 3 January 1941 at the First Battle of Bardia.

18. Paraphrase of praise given to Major General Stephen Day DSC, AM, who served in the Australian Army for over 40 years. He fought in conflicts in Africa, East Timor, Iraq and Afghanistan, with the leadership roles of Deputy Operations Officer for the Multi-National Force in Iraq, and Chief of Plans for the ISAFJoint Command in Afghanistan. He was awarded the Distinguished Service Cross (DSC), Member of the Order of Australia (AM), and appointed twice as an officer of the U.S. Legion of Merit. Formally recognised for his leadership by the Australian, French and United States governments, he is currently the State President of RSL Queensland.

    After a year fighting in Afghanistan, Major General Day's US colleagues gave him a farewell gift upon which was engraved:

    "Many young soldiers fight valiantly inside those blue lines that officers draw on maps, and some will die. You never forgot that."

    Although it was a remark meant for him, it was one that they believed distinguished all Australian generals.

19. Paraphrase of Field Marshall Erwin Rommel who said this after the 2nd Battle of El Alamein in Egypt October 23 – November 4, 1942.
20. Paraphrase of Menzies' words: *We cannot leave Greece in the lurch.*
21. This was actually said by Captain Gordon Smith of the 2/3 Regiment.
22. Paraphrase of Captain Laybourne-Smith Australian's 2/3 Field Regiment's account of the beginning of Battle of Vevi.

23. Paraphrase of Peter Ewer and his *Forgotten Anzac's* account of Private William *Bill" Jenkins. He was part of Australia's 2/3 Infantry Battalion,16 Brigade, which at the Battle of Bardia, set the stage for subsequent actions in the North African campaign, including the capture of Tobruk. Its men, then in Greece, played a crucial part in the delaying action at Tempe Gorge.
24. Quotation from Peter Ewer: *Forgotten Anzacs.*
25. Paraphrase of interview with Nurse Edwards, as cited by Peter Ewer: *Forgotten Anzacs.*
26. Paraphrase of Peter Ewer: *Forgotten Anzacs.*
27. Paraphrase of Peter Ewer: *Forgotten Anzacs.*
28. Paraphrase of Report on Action by Jais Battle Gp at Thermopylaie. German Army documents on that campaign in Greece. As cited by Peter Ewer: *Forgotten Anzacs* Kindle location: 3774.
29. Paraphrase of Peter Ewer: *Forgotten Anzacs.*
30. Captain Gwynne William (Dick) Mann, 2/1st Battalion AIF was actually awarded the Military Cross for his actions at the Battle of Bardia in Libya in January 1941. He was seriously wounded again during the fighting on Crete at the Battle of Retimo and subsequently had a leg amputated. He was treated in a German Military hospital in Athens as a POW, along with other members of his unit before being transferred to Stalag IX A, in Germany. In 1943 he was repatriated to Australia as part of an International Red Cross administered exchange of seriously sick and injured POWs. He, and his father, Captain George Nicholas Mann, who served in WWI, are Australia's only father and son Military Cross recipients.

31. Vasey's precise words were: "*To include his boy is just too terrible. He has lost a lot of caste on account of it.*"
32. A significant number of Australian troops, especially the RAAF, continued fighting with the Allied forces in Europe and the Middle East, with their airmen playing a significant role in Bomber Command's Offensive against Germany.
33. Poetic Licence. David Margesson was the Secretary of State for War. These are not his words.
34. Australia's 16th and 17th Brigades were diverted to Ceylon.
35. The 2/2 and 2/3 Battalions from Australia's 7th Division were sent to Batavia.
36. Brigadier Vasey's actual words in regard to Rowell being recalled were: *'Isn't it just too awful. I consider it a tragedy for the AIF and for Syd too. As you know he didn't see much of the last show [First World War] and here he is being defeated this time.'*
37. Paraphrase of Dudley McCarthy, Australian Official Historian's account of the Kokoda Campaign.
38. While commanding the 39th Australian Infantry Battalion, which was opposing the enemy advance, Lieutenant Colonel Owen, although facing far superior numbers of enemy troops, directed his men so effectively as to extract a heavy toll on the enemy forces and considerably delay their advance. His courageous and inspiring personal example was in great measure responsible for this vigorous opposition to the enemy attack. Lieutenant Colonel Owen was seriously wounded in this action and later died of his wounds
39. Private Bruce Kingsbury of the 2/14 Australian Infantry Battalion. On 29 August 1942, during the Battle of Isurava,

Kingsbury was one of the few survivors of a platoon that had been overrun by the Japanese. He immediately volunteered to join a different platoon, which had been ordered to counter-attack. Rushing forward and firing his Bren gun from the hip, he cleared a path through the enemy and inflicted several casualties. Kingsbury was then shot by a sniper and killed instantly. His actions, which delayed the Japanese long enough for the Australians to fortify their positions, were instrumental in saving his battalion's headquarters.

40. Paraphrase of Lieutenant Colonel Ralph Honner's famous speech to the men of his 39th Battalion at Menari village (Kokoda Trail) on 6 September 1942.
41. Jack Beasley was a member of the Australian Labor Party and government minister in both Curtin and Chifley's governments. He served in the Australian War Cabinet from 1941-46.
42. This letter from Rowell was not written to Lavarack but to Major General Cyril Clowes at Milne Bay.
43. Sir Keith Murdoch was Chairman of the Herald and Weekly Times newspaper.
44. Paraphrased account of the Battle of Ioribaiwa given by Sergeant Eric Williams of the 2/16 Battalion.
45. Paraphrased account of the Battle of Ioribaiwa given by Captain Bill Grayden of the 2/16 Battalion.
46. This was at the Koitaki Plantation 24 miles from Port Moresby.
47. H.S. Foll (Hattil Spencer "Harry" Foll) was an Australian Senator for Queensland from 1917 to 1947, a member of the

Nationalist, United Australia, and Liberal parties. He served as a Minister for Repatriation, Health, Interior and Information during his career and was a World War I veteran who was wounded at Gallipoli.

48. For his service during the First World War, Lavarack was awarded the Distinguished Service Order (1918) and the French Croix de Guerre (1919). He was appointed a Companion of the Order of St Michael and St. George in 1919 and Mentioned in Despatches three times. In 1942, following I Corps' actions in the Syria-Lebanon Campaign, he was appointed a Knight Commander of the Order of the British Empire (KBE). He was appointed a Knight Commander of the Royal Victorian Order in 1954 and a Knight Commander of the Order of St Michael and St George.
49. Vasey went by either of his Christian names, but was more generally known as Alan.
50. This question wasn't asked by MacArthur at the specified social function, but by another.
51. Paraphrase of Sir John Lavarack in interview with journalist and military historian Gavin Long.
52. Much of this Berryman epilogue is a paraphrase of Peter Dean's university thesis on Berryman. Professor Peter J. Dean PhD SFHEA is the Director, Foreign Policy and Defence at the United States Studies Centre at the University of Sydney.
53. Paraphrase of Curtin"s statement published on 28 December in the Sydney Daily Telegraph.
54. Paraphrase of Edwards.
55. Paraphrase of Presbyterian minister, Hector Harrison.

56. Paraphrase of Gavin Long.
57. Paraphrase of Keith Murdoch.
58. Military historian, Peter Brune.

www.ingramcontent.com/pod-product-compliance
Lightning Source LLC
LaVergne TN
LVHW091035080826
845145LV00002B/511